Cam Pratt was kissing her!

And she was kissing him back.

It didn't matter that his face was stubbly after their long day's work. It only mattered that his lips were parted and sweet, his breath was soft against her skin, his hand was firm but gentle on her face. And, oh, could the man kiss! It was no wonder he'd been so popular in high school....

Then it was over and she had to force herself not to strain for another one, to accept that that single kiss was going to be it.

For now...

Dear Reader,

Growing up the ugly-duckling brainiac of small-town Northbridge, Montana, Eden Perry was, unsurprisingly, the brunt of hurtful teasing. So when I started to think about her, I pictured a sort of victim. But that's when things took a turn and I realized that she might have fought back. And that in fighting back, she might have struck out at someone who didn't deserve it, and ended up feeling terribly guilty about it. Guilty enough that it might put a damper on returning to her hometown even though she looks a whole lot better than she did once upon a time. And if the person who didn't deserve the harsh treatment she'd dished out just happened to be the drop-dead-gorgeous guy she now has to work with? Hmm, that just might have some possibilities....

That's how *Hometown Cinderella* came to be. And while Eden doesn't have the help of a fairy godmother, she could use one when it comes to facing our angry, wishes-he-never-had-to-lay-eyes-on-her-again hero. I think it makes for some fun for those of us looking in on them, though. I hope you agree.

Happy reading!

Victoria Pade

HOMETOWN CINDERELLA

VICTORIA PADE

Silhouette

SPECIAL EDITION

Published by Silhouette Books

America's Publisher of Contemporary Romance

 SILHOUETTE BOOKS

ISBN-13: 978-0-373-24804-9
ISBN-10:   0-373-24804-0

HOMETOWN CINDERELLA

Visit Silhouette Books at www.eHarlequin.com

Printed in U.S.A.

Books by Victoria Pade

Silhouette Special Edition

VICTORIA PADE

is a native of Colorado, where she continues to live and work. Her passion—besides writing—is chocolate, which she indulges in frequently and in every form. She loves romance novels and romantic movies—the more lighthearted, the better—but she likes a good, juicy mystery now and then, too.

Chapter One

"She's here…"

Cam Pratt was in the break room of the police station. His shift had just ended and he'd brought his coffee mug in to wash when Luke Walker poked his head through a crack in the door to make his announcement.

Cam pumped some soap into the mug and glanced over his shoulder at his friend and fellow officer. "Who's here?"

Luke Walker grinned. "Eden Perry."

Cam screwed up his face and groaned. "Now?"

"Right now. She just walked in the door. She wants to take a look at the computer setup she'll be using."

"It's four-thirty and you're on duty, I'm not. You show it to her," Cam said, hoping for an out.

"Uh-uh. You know it's already been decided that this is your baby. Even if it means working with someone you have some leftover high school hang-up about for reasons you don't want to say. And since I caught you before you left…"

Cam curled his upper lip like a fractious hound dog. Then he said, "I'll be there in a minute."

"You won't recognize her," Luke threw in just before he disappeared from the doorway and closed the door.

Cam couldn't have cared less if he recognized Eden Perry or not. The little pain-in-the-ass—

He cut his own thought short, knowing that recalling the past would only piss him off. As it did every time he thought about it. Or about Eden Perry. Every time he'd thought about her since learning before the holidays that he'd be overseeing the work of the former hometown girl and forensic artist when she arrived.

But he'd already tried convincing his superior officer to let him steer clear of this portion of an investigation that had been ongoing for months now and it hadn't done him any good. Luke was right—this was his baby.

Whether he liked it or not.

Whether he liked Eden Perry or not.

And he didn't like Eden Perry. Or having to be anywhere around her, let alone work with her. In fact, when he'd returned to the small town of Northbridge, Montana, two years ago, he'd been happy to learn that Eden Perry had left for college shortly after he had and had rarely even visited since then.

But apparently things had changed for her and now here she was—back to live and hired to do an age-progression of the woman who had become the focal point of an old case that also happened to be the biggest scandal ever to rock Northbridge. And, to make matters worse, Eden Perry was also his neighbor.

"Which is why you decided to try to tolerate her, remember?" he told himself as he pumped more soap into his mug because he'd forgotten he'd already done it.

Not that he regretted repeating a step. He sure as hell wasn't in any hurry to go out to the person he would have just as soon never set eyes on again.

But he didn't have that option and he knew it.

On the other hand, he thought, the sooner he got this going, the sooner he could be finished with it. Finished with working with Eden Perry, even if he couldn't be finished with living right next door to her.

But finishing with at least one thing to do with her was better than nothing, he reasoned.

And maybe after this they could just ignore each other.

"But so help me, if she shoots off her mouth I don't care who she is or how lucky we are to have her do this, I'll blow her right out of the water," he muttered as he finally turned on the faucet and began to scrub his coffee cup with a punishing fervor.

"You'll be working with Cam Pratt," Luke Walker told Eden as she stood waiting in the outer office of the police station. "I don't know if you remember him—"

"I remember him," Eden said, not thrilled with that news. At all.

"From high school," Luke Walker seemed inclined to say anyway. "You two graduated the same year, didn't you? I know you started out in my class but then you were skipped ahead, right?"

"Right," she confirmed a bit stiltedly. She hadn't

been—or felt—stiff before. It had just happened at the mention of Cam Pratt. And at the idea that she'd be working with him.

"I didn't know he was on the force," she said then. "Or even in Northbridge. Last I heard he didn't live here."

"He moved back a couple of years ago."

"Ah," Eden said as if it were an irrelevant revelation when, in fact, she had to fight the urge to recoil. "Is there a particular reason I'll be working with Cam and not with you or someone else?"

"Yeah, Cam was a cop in the heart of Detroit for a long time. He's had experience with the kind of stuff you do but this will be a first for the rest of us, so he was the logical choice."

Eden nodded, hating that she was so on edge suddenly and at a loss for anything else to say to Luke Walker now that her mind was spinning in a different direction.

"I just came on duty," Luke said then, into the awkward silence she'd left. "I should get out, do my first patrol…."

"It's okay, you don't have to stay on my account. Go ahead."

"Cam will be right out. He just finished for the day so he's wrapping up a few things. I'm sure he'll only be another minute. Why don't you have a seat at his desk? It's the one facing mine."

Eden nodded again but didn't sit. She was too lost in thinking that of course Cam Pratt didn't hesitate to leave her cooling her heels. After all, she was an inconsequential little nobody and he was probably still hot stuff just the way he'd been then. The Man. The guy every senior girl—except Eden—had wanted to end up with. It shouldn't have come as any surprise that he would appear when he deigned to appear and not before. As if he were doing her a favor, which he probably thought he was—

Eden put the brakes on her runaway thoughts, shocked to have so instantly reverted to what would have gone through her head in this instance fourteen years ago.

But this wasn't fourteen years ago....

"Are you okay? You're kind of flushed all of a sudden," Luke Walker said then.

He must have been waiting for her to take the seat he'd offered because he hadn't moved, either. But she'd been oblivious to him and his voice drew her out of her reverie.

She pressed the fingertips of one hand to her cheek, feeling the increased heat of her skin. "It's a little warm in here. Maybe the coat's too much inside."

"And maybe you *should* sit down," he suggested again.

As she slipped off her camel hair jacket and went to hang it over the back of the chair he'd indicated she said, "I'm fine. Go ahead out on patrol. There's no reason for you to stick around. Really. It's not as if I'm a stranger to cop shops."

Luke Walker acknowledged that with a raise of his chin but even as he went to the coatrack for his own jacket he kept an eye on her.

Was she making a fool of herself?

She hoped not.

It was just so amazing how one mention of Cam Pratt could send her right back to high school. Right back to being the geeky, braces-on-her-teeth, glasses-wearing, frizzy-haired, flat-chested brainiac in a grade she might have belonged in academically, but certainly hadn't belonged in socially. Right back to where she'd been made fun of on a daily basis and then suddenly thrust into dealing with the big-man-on-campus himself. One-on-one.

And she hadn't dealt with it well. Or in a way that she was proud of.

In fact, it embarrassed her to recall that time in her life. The time she'd spent with Cam Pratt. And how she'd behaved.

"I think maybe I'll use your restroom," she said suddenly, wanting to escape Luke Walker's continuing scrutiny from across the room as he seemed to be stalling his departure. Besides, she needed a moment to get a grip on herself.

"The ladies' room is down the hall," he informed her, pointing with his thumb.

"Great. Thanks. Nice to see you again," she said, subtly encouraging him to leave as she headed in the direction he'd indicated.

"Yeah, you, too," Luke Walker called after her, giving no indication whether or not he would be on his way once she was out of sight.

Although maybe it would be better if he didn't leave, she thought as she found the restroom and went in. Maybe it would be better if she had a buffer when she had to face Cam Pratt.

Cam Pratt.

She was going to have to work with Cam Pratt. She let that thought sink in as she closed the restroom door behind her.

Cam Pratt, of all people.

No crime goes unpunished....

Not that she'd committed an actual crime against

him. But she had been wretched toward him. Wretched enough to be ashamed of herself.

Maybe he doesn't remember, she thought hopefully. Maybe to him it was nothing. No big deal. Not worthy of recall any more than I was worthy of notice....

That seemed possible—that this was a bigger thing in her own memory than it had been to him. After all, he'd been a supreme being in high school and she'd been a complete and total nobody. A nonentity. He probably didn't even remember *her,* let alone anything that she might have said to him so long ago. She was probably making a mountain out of a molehill.

This was a new day. A new page. A new chapter. And she should just take things as they came and not go in expecting the worst.

Even if that wasn't altogether easy for her when old insecurities reared their ugly head. When offense just instinctively felt like the best form of defense the way it had fourteen years ago.

But things had changed. *She'd* changed, she reminded herself. And to reinforce that reminder she moved to the sole sink in the single-stall restroom to have a glimpse of the present-day Eden Perry.

Because lo and behold, the geek was gone.

No more braces—her teeth were completely straight now.

No more glasses—contacts had replaced them a decade ago and eye surgery had removed even the need for those more recently, so her ice-blue eyes were only adorned with mascara.

Her skin had cleared; in fact, there wasn't a single blemish or red mark marring it. Instead it was smooth and creamy and even-toned with just a little blush to brighten it.

She'd grown into her arms and legs. And her head——thank goodness! Nothing was out of proportion the way it had been when she'd been all elbows and knees and skinny, scrawny body.

Her bustline had developed—there was no question that she was female now, she could fill out a bra with the best of them. Well, with the best of the B-cups, anyway.

Her hair had darkened to a burnt-sienna red—no one had called her pumpkinhead in fourteen years. And the relaxer she used eased the kinky curls into mere waves that she could keep manageable at shoulder length.

So all in all, no, she wasn't odd-looking anymore. There was no reason she would be called names or taunted or teased or tormented. And she didn't have to go into any situation armed for those kinds of battles.

A new day. A new page. A new chapter.

That was what she needed to keep in mind. And that Cam Pratt had likely been unaffected by the bad attitude of the mousy nerd-girl he hadn't had any reason to think twice about when he was on top of the world. Or probably since.

Eden tugged at the collar of the white shirt she was wearing underneath a beige cardigan sweater. Then she made sure the shirt was neatly-tucked into the tan slacks she had on. Finally, she stood a little straighter, surveying the whole picture and deciding that then and now were totally different on every front.

This would be okay, she told herself. Fourteen years was a long time. Anything that had happened that far in the past was ancient history….

Except that when she left the bathroom a few minutes later and returned to the main office, every bit of that reassurance went right out the window.

What had she thought? That Cam Pratt might not remember her or how she'd treated him? That he probably hadn't been affected?

Think again...

Because there he was, waiting for her.

And if ever Eden had seen anyone whose expression said he bore a grudge against her, it was Cam Pratt.

She stood frozen at the mouth of the hallway that had led her from the restroom to the main portion of the office, brought up short by the hard stare of the six-foot-two-inch man she had been cruel to once upon a time.

But what was she going to do? She asked herself. She couldn't run the other way. So she took a deep breath to steady herself and managed to cross to where he was leaning one broad shoulder against the wall near the fingerprinting station, his arms clasped over a noteworthy chest encased in his dark blue uniform.

"Cam?" she said, making a firm but quiet question of his name despite the fact that there was no doubt who he was. Even if he had somehow matured into a more colossally handsome specimen than he'd been the last time she'd seen him—something she didn't want to be aware of.

The not-bushy but slightly unruly eyebrows that matched his dark, dark brown hair pulled together only enough to let her know he was surprised by the updated version of her as he gave her a quick once-over. But unlike the approval Luke Walker had voiced when she'd first let him know who she was, Cam Pratt seemed unimpressed by the improvements. He only answered with a flat and contempt-filled "Eden."

"Yes," she confirmed, although it was just to have something to say.

And then it struck her that she didn't know where to go from there. Since he obviously remembered her and how things had been fourteen years ago, she wondered if she should offer a long-overdue apology. Should she tell him she knew she'd been horrible? That in hindsight she regretted it?

But somehow when she imagined doing that it seemed to have the potential for making things even more awkward than they already were. And things were already so awkward there was a palpable tension in the air. So maybe it was better to just go from here....

She squared her shoulders and adopted the purely professional demeanor she'd used on many occasions going in to work with people she didn't know and merely said, "I'm sorry to keep you when you were ready to leave for the day. I just wanted to see the computer I'll be using to make sure it has the capabilities I'll need. And if you wouldn't mind, I'd be interested to hear where this case stands and what exactly you're hoping I can do."

"I've been ordered to be at your disposal—whenever and wherever—so I guess it's your prerogative to keep me late."

"Prerogative or not, I won't do it again," she said, formally but politely, refusing to let his antagonistic tone echo in hers. "In the future I'll be sure I come in during your work hours."

"Uh-huh, well, I guess we'll see, won't we?" he said

with disbelief before he pushed off the wall and nodded toward a door. "The computer you need is in here," he said, throwing open the door and indicating that she should lead the way.

He was just determined not to be nice. Determined for the shoe to be on the other foot, Eden thought.

But as she went through that door and entered the small room beyond it she told herself his disgust was no less than she deserved and she decided to ignore what he seemed bent on dishing out.

He followed her into the cubicle-sized space. There were computers on the office desks but the setup in this room was larger.

"I checked," he said once they were both standing in front of the machines. "This should meet all of your requirements, memory and otherwise."

"Good," Eden said, glad for the opportunity to look at something other than him as she scanned for the options she liked to have available for visual imagining. In spite of his assurance.

"Right, check for yourself. I'm sure I can't be trusted to know what I'm doing."

"I just wanted to make certain there was a scanner and that I can connect a camera if I need to."

He sighed audibly, as if he were keeping a tight hold on his temper. But he made no other comment. Instead, obviously in a hurry to get this over with, he obliged the second request she'd made of him by relaying the facts of the case she'd be working on. "As you know, we're looking for Celeste Perry—"

"My grandmother," Eden supplied, satisfied with the computer and glancing at Cam once more.

"What we know," he continued, "is that Mickey Rider and Frank Dorian robbed the Northbridge bank in 1960. A duffel bag containing the belongings of Mickey Rider was found in the rafters of the old north bridge a few months ago. Stains on the bag were confirmed to be a match for Rider's blood and after a search for his body, human remains were discovered in the woods not far from the bridge."

Cam's words couldn't have been more clipped but Eden preferred that to sarcasm. For some reason she didn't understand, however, she was having difficulty concentrating on much more than the color of eyes that were so deep a blue they were almost black.

"Those remains have been examined," he was saying, "and conclusively identified as those of Rider, with a blow to the head the apparent cause of death. Frank Dorian—the man Celeste left town with—was arrested by the FBI several months after the robbery and was killed in an escape attempt before he ever got to trial. Because both robbers are now known to be deceased—and Rider possibly murdered—and since the robbery money has never been recovered, there's renewed interest in Celeste."

"Is there suspicion that *she* murdered Rider?" Eden managed to ask when she forced herself to focus on what he was telling her rather than on the scruffy five-o'clock shadow that dusted the lower half of a face that somehow managed to be rugged and refined at the same time.

"I won't say Celeste *isn't* a murder suspect," he answered. "When the FBI had Dorian in custody and questioned him, he contended that your grandmother had had no part in the robbery, but since he was claiming at the time that his partner had taken half the money and gone off on his own, there was no indication that Rider was dead or whether or not Celeste was involved. Now everything is in question again."

"And at the very least Celeste could have been an accessory before or after the fact," Eden contributed even as she cataloged the length and shape of his nose—a little long with a bit of a bump in the bridge that was somehow sexy....

"Like I said, there's renewed interest in Celeste," he repeated.

"And my part in this?" Eden prompted, fighting to keep her thoughts where they belonged and not on him.

"When Dorian was questioned he claimed that Celeste had gained considerable weight, plus there's a woman in Bozeman who believes she might have worked with Celeste in 1968. We have a description from her for you to work into the whole picture and she also described Celeste as heavyset—"

"Celeste...my grandmother...was as near as Bozeman? I hadn't heard that," Eden said, shocked and yanked by that shock from studying his sideburns—not too long, not too short.

"Yes, it seems likely your grandmother was in Bozeman and calling herself Charlotte Pierce. Does that ring a bell?"

Eden shook her head. "No, the name Charlotte Pierce doesn't sound familiar," she said. "And I'm sure my family told you when they were dispatched to ask, but I don't ever remember having any contact with anyone who might have been Celeste, either. Or with anyone who caused any kind of question in my mind."

"That information was relayed and entered into the reports," he confirmed. "But between the weight gain and the fact that a lot of years have passed to also alter Celeste's appearance, we thought a computer image progression might help to approximate the changes as she aged, along with what she might look like now. If we can, we want to determine if she ever did come back to or through Northbridge again—the way she told several people she planned in order to see her sons again—"

"My dad and my uncle," Eden said even as her gaze drifted to Cam's wavy hair worn just long enough to be combed back on top and short everywhere else.

But they were talking about her grandmother's appearance, she reminded herself, not Cam's.

"So I'll have the description from the woman in Bozeman," she said then, "and what else? There can't be many photographs of Celeste—*I've* never seen one."

"Because your grandfather destroyed them all when she took off. The only picture we have of her is from the newspaper article written when she and the reverend moved to town. She was in her twenties in the snapshot and showing it around hasn't done any good. We're hoping that whatever you come up with will be more what she might have looked like later on and may spur someone's memory. If Celeste did come through here she might have left behind some clue as to where she was headed after that, where she might be now if she's still alive."

"Or if she came into Northbridge and stayed—my sisters and cousins told me there's speculation about that."

"Some," Cam conceded. "And that's it. That's where the case stands. Except that we're getting pressure from the FBI and from the state investigators to get things moving on this. The skeletal remains were found at the start of November. Between waiting for the results from forensics and the holiday holdups, and then waiting for you to get here, the last two months and counting have just gone down the drain."

He said that as if it were entirely Eden's fault and made her feel the need to justify herself.

"I was working on another case before Christmas and then I had to get back to Hawaii to pack up my house—my whole life really—and arrange to get everything here. I just arrived this morning, driving my car behind the moving van. I had to wait for the truck to be unloaded and as soon as it was, I came here because I know this needs to get underway. If there was too much of a rush to wait for me, you could have had someone else do this for you. It isn't even my official job anymore, I've quit to do other things and only agreed to do this one last case because I'd be in Northbridge anyway and it seemed dumb to make anyone else come in to do it."

"You *are* the authority on dumb," he said under his breath.

No, he hadn't forgotten a thing....

"And I suppose," he added facetiously before she could respond to his comment, "that you aren't curious about any of this yourself."

Not even disgust disguised the suppleness of lips that were perfectly shaped.

"Of course I'm curious," Eden said. "I have a personal interest—this is my grandmother. The woman who ran out on my grandfather and abandoned my father and my uncle when they were little boys. And then to think that there's any possibility that she's actually been here, that I could have run into her at some point or even know her? Yes, I'm anxious to do this job and see who my grandmother might be. But what I'm saying is—"

"Yeah, I know what you're saying—that there's something in it for you but that we should still be grateful to have you."

He might not be hard on the eyes but he definitely wasn't going to make this easy.

"No, what I'm saying is that I got here as soon as I could but if that wasn't good enough, you didn't need to wait for me."

"Apparently we did," he nearly sneered.

Again Eden reminded herself that he had cause to dislike her and bypassed his less-than-subtle display of it. "Well, I'm here now and I'll get this done. Although probably not before Wednesday because I'll need a day to get myself organized enough to find the box with my equipment and software—"

"I'm just glad to hear you don't want to do it this minute. I'd like to get home."

In other words, he didn't care about her explanation, he only wanted this meeting finished.

Eden was more than willing to oblige him—a feast for the eyes or not, she was hardly enjoying this.

"I've seen what I came to see, I think we're done here," she informed him.

"Does that mean I'm *dismissed?*"

"It just means we're done for now," she said with a weary sigh.

"Good," he decreed, walking out of the small room just like that. Without another word or a backward glance.

Maybe he had some of that stuff fourteen years ago coming, Eden thought, losing her patience as she trailed behind to return to the outer office.

He put on his coat in silence.

Eden put on her coat in silence.

And they both arrived at the door at the same time.

"After you," he said none too nicely, sweeping a long arm toward the station entrance.

Eden took a breath and held it in order to stay her tongue, preceding him out the door and paying him no attention as she went to her compact car parked in the small lot behind the police station.

Of course, as luck would have it, she was nose to nose with his SUV.

Eden pretended not to notice.

He started his engine.

She started her engine.

And they both arrived at the lot exit at the same time.

Eden motioned for Cam to go ahead of her.

He did, turning right onto South Street.

Eden turned right onto South Street.

He went past Main Street and so did she.

He turned right three blocks after that.

And so did she.

"Oh, don't tell me…" She moaned a split second before he pulled into one side of the double driveway she shared with her next-door neighbor to the north and she pulled into the other side.

Neck and neck they drove to the matching garages that were separated from each other by mere feet at the rear of the properties.

Eden came to a stop in front of hers.

Cam stopped in front of what was apparently his.

Eden got out of her car.

Cam got out of his SUV.

And they arrived at the rear of their vehicles at the same time.

"You live next door?" she asked, trying to keep her distaste out of her voice. And failing.

He arched an eyebrow. "Nobody told you?"

"No. In fact, I was told someone named Poppazitto owned that house."

"Right. But I'm renting the place from the Poppazittos with an option to buy when the lease expires in two months."

"So we're neighbors," Eden said, lamenting the fact more to herself than to him.

"Neighbors, but not friends," he countered, turning on his heel and once again presenting his back to her as he walked away.

And even if it was a very, very fine back, Eden had to fight the inordinate urge to pick up a rock and aim for it.

Chapter Two

Cam had done his usual morning workout before he'd gone on duty. But he knew if he didn't work *off* some of what Eden Perry had riled up in him he'd never be able to relax, let alone sleep that night. So about eight o'clock he went out the back door of his house and braved the cold January air to cross his yard to the garage.

Both his and Eden's houses and garages had originally been built by identical twin brothers who had designed the ranch-style houses and the garages to be as much alike as the brothers themselves. Which meant that both garages were single-car sized with a second story containing very small studio apartments. Each apartment was comprised of an open space for a combined living room-bedroom, a tiny bathroom, and a bare-basics kitchen made up of a few cupboards, a sink and a section that could accommodate a refrigerator and a stove.

Cam had had plans to buy the house, garage and apartment at the end of his lease, figuring to eventually add the now-missing stove and refrigerator, and rent the place to a college kid for some extra income. Until then, it was a decent spot for his weights and other gym equipment.

But after spending even a small amount of time that afternoon with Eden Perry he thought he should reconsider buying the place at all and being right next door to her indefinitely.

He wasn't sure he was going to be able to even live out the next two months of the lease so near to Her Royal Highness The Mighty Forensic Artist.

He slung the towel he'd brought with him over the stand that held his weights, and stripped off his sweats so he was only in gym shorts and a T-shirt. Then he started to do his second warm-up of the day, hoping that exercise would get Eden Perry out of his head. Because that's where she'd been since the first minute he'd set eyes on her at the station today.

If there were any justice in the world, he thought as he stretched his calf muscles, she would have stayed looking the way she had when she was a teenager—hair that had been such a bright orange and so stick-out-everywhere curly that it had looked as if it belonged on a clown wig, glasses as thick as the bottoms of mayonnaise jars, braces imprisoning crooked teeth, bad skin and a body that had been as flat as a pancake with only knobby knees and pointy elbows to give her any shape at all.

Her homeliness had helped him make it through that miserable time he'd had to spend with her fourteen years ago. He'd figured that it served her right, that it was a warning of what was below the surface—foul on the outside, foul on the inside. It had seemed fitting.

But now?

Hell, now she was so damn gorgeous his mouth had nearly dropped open when she'd stopped at the end of that hallway coming back into the office.

And that *didn't* seem fair....

Sufficiently warmed up, he got down on the floor for sit-ups. But that still didn't allow him an escape from thinking about Eden Perry.

Her hair wasn't orange anymore, now it was the color of Colorado's red rocks when they were drenched with spring rain—a deep, warm, fresh lobster hue. And the kinky curl? That had calmed down to thick, shiny waves that fell to her shoulders.

It didn't frame a splotchy, zitty face any longer, either. Her teenage blemishes had cleared and what she had left was skin like the petals of a pale pink rose. Dewy, soft-looking skin over high cheekbones, a delicate nose and a facial structure that had somehow blossomed into a kind of subtle elegance.

Damn her, anyway.

The braces had apparently done their job, too, because her teeth were straight. And gleaming white behind lips that were no longer chapped and uninviting. Lips that had the barest blush to them and were anything but uninviting....

He picked up the speed on the sit-ups.

But no matter how fast and furious he did them, the mental image of Eden kept assaulting him.

He'd been shocked to see her eyes. He guessed he'd never noticed them when they'd been hidden behind the lenses of her glasses. But when she'd raised them to him that afternoon? It had been hard to believe he could have ever missed them. They were blue—like a clear summer sky—but they were like looking at that clear blue sky through frosted crystal. They almost seemed transparent. And coupled with that hair? Geez, she was a knockout.

He flipped over and started doing push-ups even faster than he'd done sit-ups, counting them aloud in hopes that that would distract him from thinking about Eden. From picturing her.

But did it?

No, it didn't. At number thirty-one it occurred to him that that was Eden's age. And that her thirty-one-year-old body was better than it had been, too. Not centerfold better, but definitely better enough that he hadn't been aware of her elbows or knees. Instead he'd noticed that she was a tight, compact little package, with just enough up-front. Just enough to draw his interest. More than once.

Yeah, if Eden Perry wasn't the transformation of the century, he didn't know what was.

On the outside.

But what about the inside? That probably hadn't changed, he thought with some satisfaction.

The satisfaction was short-lived, however, because when he tried to think of how her bad disposition had displayed itself he couldn't come up with anything.

He'd been the one with the bad disposition today. She hadn't acted the way she had when they were teenagers, and he reluctantly—*very* reluctantly—admitted that.

Of course she also hadn't been warm and friendly.

But then neither had he.

He'd been rude and obnoxious, if the truth be told. And she hadn't even shot back at him.

How come? he wondered suddenly.

That sure as hell wasn't the old Eden Perry. The old Eden Perry would have shot first. And barring that, she would certainly have returned fire. Hell, the Eden Perry he'd known would have mounted a savage counterattack.

But the Eden Perry he'd known had also been sixteen years old, he thought—again for no reason he understood. Sixteen years old and as ugly as a mud fence. And this Eden Perry wasn't either of those things anymore.

So, what if she also wasn't the rude, mouthy, insulting, aggravating nightmare she'd been before, either?

That would be hard to believe!

But somehow the possibility slowed his push-ups and eventually brought them to a stop.

Was it possible Eden Perry was different outside and inside? he asked himself as he moved on to the weight bench for a few biceps curls.

Eden Perry different…

Huh.

Did he buy that? Did he buy the all-business version she'd been today? Kind of wooden but not nasty or mean-spirited or bitchy?

He didn't know. He supposed that he could concede that she might—just *might*—have learned to curb her tongue in the course of growing up.

But so what? he asked himself. Did that mean that she thought of *him* any differently than she had when they were kids?

Probably not.

And given that, did he want anything more to do

with her than he had when he'd been expecting that sharp tongue to fly out and cut him like a razor blade?

No, he didn't.

Even if she was something pretty eye-popping to look at.

He'd still keep his distance, thanks just the same, he thought.

Because eye-popping or not, better behaved or not, there was one thing Eden Perry had made clear enough to him when she was sixteen—she thought he was an idiot.

And the last thing he needed—or wanted—was to be within a hundred yards of any woman who thought of him as someone dumber than a doorknob.

No matter how she looked.

But damn, Eden Perry *did* look good....

Eden had changed her clothes and gone right to work on her bedroom when she returned from the police station.

By about 8:30 that night she had located her mattress pad, sheets, blankets, pillows and quilt, and made her bed so she would have a place to sleep. She'd hung shades and curtains on both bedroom windows and put most of her clothes in the closet. She'd filled the underwear drawer of her dresser and unpacked all the toiletries she would need to start the next day.

And while it may have been only 8:30, she'd been up since before dawn, driven for two hours to reach Northbridge, overseen the three movers unloading her things, and then she'd had that unpleasant encounter with Cam Pratt *before* laboring all evening, too. She was tired and hungry and ready to drop.

So she went into the kitchen in search of food,

grateful that her sister Eve had stocked it with a few things to tide her over until she could do some shopping.

Weaving through boxes stacked everywhere, including on her kitchen table, she opened the refrigerator. Eggs, butter and cream for her coffee were its sole occupants.

She hadn't located her pots and pans yet but she knew where to find a bowl so she could scramble an egg in the microwave. But she decided to check the pantry first.

Bread, cheese puffs—her sister knew her well— and Chinese noodle soup already in its own microwavable cup.

She opted for the soup because it was the simplest of all to prepare.

With cup in hand, she went to the sink to fill it with water. When she reached the sink her gaze automatically drifted out the window above it and went instantly to the garages nestled so close together in back.

Only it wasn't her own garage that caught her attention. It was Cam Pratt's. Specifically, the light that was shining through the undraped window in the space over the garage.

She knew that that space in her own outbuilding was a makeshift apartment. She intended to use it as an art studio. But she didn't know if it was also an apartment in the other garage and if that was rented out, too, to someone other than Cam Pratt.

So she stood rooted to the spot, staring at the large rectangular window that matched hers, hoping to catch a glimpse of whoever was up there.

She didn't have long to wait.

Within moments she saw Cam Pratt cross in front of the window and go to some kind of bar that seemed to be jammed into the doorway that led to what would have been the bathroom in her unit.

Because she was looking from a ground floor level through a second floor window, she could only see the top portions of the above-the-garage room and of the man who was in it. But that was enough to give her a glimpse of him from behind, reaching long, well-muscled arms upward and grasping the bar—palms towards him—in his huge hands.

As she watched, he began to use the bar to do pull-ups and with each one his full back and waist came into view.

Now that she knew she didn't have yet another neighbor, what went on in that room shouldn't have been of any further interest to Eden. But she couldn't seem to tear herself away. Or so much as look at anything else. Instead, she stayed right where she was, eyes trained on that second floor window in the distance.

Cam was wearing a plain white T-shirt that clung damply to his broad shoulders and the V of his back where it narrowed to his waist. And although the shirt concealed the details of what it encased, the powerful swell of his arms from the short sleeves gave her a clue as to what was going on within the shirt, too. And it was noteworthy.

She was aware that cops were encouraged to keep in shape and apparently Cam Pratt took that seriously. Because he was in very, very good shape as he raised and lowered himself from that bar at the same rate her heart was beating. As if they were somehow in sync.

Up and down. Up and down. Her eyes lingered on that back. On those biceps flexing, bulging within glistening skin that seemed barely able to contain them. Up and down and up again…

The man had stamina, she'd give him that.

Stamina and strength and a fabulous physique that she had some kind of irrational urge to get closer to. To touch. To test for herself if those muscles were as solid and unyielding as they looked.

It doesn't matter, she told herself firmly.

Because regardless of how he looked, he had two strikes against him and she was determined not to forget either of them. Not only had he been a bear to her that afternoon in response to a history that she would rather forget—strike one—but he *was* a cop. Strike two. And she didn't want anything to do with another cop. Or with anything that put her anywhere near cops or crime or criminals.

No, doing this age progression of her long-lost grandmother was going to be her last foray into that world and then Eden was finished with it.

Absolutely finished.

But still, there Cam was, and if chin-ups were a televised sport she thought he would have been the star of the show.

Soup. Make the soup....

But did she?

No, she didn't. Instead she went on being engrossed in the sight of Cam Pratt exercising, feeling warmer and warmer herself....

He's a cop, you know what that means. And he's a jerk, too....

But a jerk with a body of steel....

She'd just watch three more....

Three. Four.

Five.

Six.

Eight.

Ten…

She was still watching when he stopped. And she went on looking even when his big hands dropped from the bar. Even when he moved out of sight. And for a few minutes after that her eyes continued to be glued to that window. Waiting. Holding her breath.

Until she realized what she was doing.

She was tired, she told herself then. She hadn't been mesmerized by watching Cam Pratt do chin-ups, she'd just hit some kind of wall of fatigue that had put her in a zombielike trance for a few minutes.

That's all it was.

A night's rest and she'd be impervious to that same display. She was sure of it.

She finally turned on the hot water and filled her soup cup.

Okay, so yes, when she had, she did glance out the window again. Once. Long enough to see that Cam had left the garage apartment and was on his way back to his house, dressed in faded red sweatpants and a white hooded sweatshirt now.

But the instant she saw him look in her direction she jolted backward, hoping he hadn't caught her gawking at him through her kitchen window.

"And if he did see you, that's what you get," she chastised herself as she headed for the microwave.

The microwave wasn't where she wanted it—it was just on the counter where the movers had left it. But she wasn't going to reposition it tonight, so she merely jabbed the button to open the door.

The door didn't respond and she stared at it, wondering if the oven had been broken in transit.

It actually took her a moment to drag her thoughts far enough away from the mental image of Cam Pratt that was still haunting her to figure out that the microwave wasn't plugged in.

"Oh, brother, you better snap out of this," she advised herself as she plugged in the appliance.

Then she put her soup cup inside and started the oven.

And that was when everything went dark.

With a weary sigh she returned to the window over the sink to see if more than her lights had gone out. They hadn't, the lights in the alley behind the garage were still on so the blackout wasn't a power outage. She'd only overloaded her own circuits.

She should have known better. Just about every light in the house had been on, her stereo had been playing, the iron was plugged in, so was her electric drill, and trying to use the microwave on top of it all must have tripped the breaker. Or blown a fuse—whichever the old house was equipped with.

Which she didn't know. Any more than she knew where the breaker box or fuse box was located.

The only illumination in the house was coming from the alley lights and it was next to nothing. She owned a flashlight but she didn't have a clue where it was and without it there was no way she would ever see the box in the basement or the attic or wherever it was.

She needed help. At the very least she needed someone to tell her where the main panel was. But who could she call to ask?

Her sister Eve was her first thought but she knew Eve

was in Billings until the next day chauffeuring their grandfather.

Her cousins weren't likely to know anything about a house none of them had ever lived in, and the previous owners had left the state immediately after the closing by proxy.

Maybe the Realtor would know.

Stumbling over packing containers and things she'd pulled out and left on the floor, she finally found her cell phone. But when she used it to dial the number she had programmed for the Realtor she only got a voice mail message that Betty would not be available Monday or Tuesday.

Which seemed to leave Eden with only one alternative.

Her house and the house next door were exactly alike.

Surely the breaker box or the fuse box was located in the same place.

And not only would Cam Pratt know where that was, he would probably have a flashlight she could borrow to find it.

Cam Pratt.

Again.

"This is just not my day," Eden grumbled.

Maybe she should forget eating and go to bed, she thought, desperate for any other alternative. She could search the place in the morning, in the daylight.

But it was the dead of winter. In Montana. And already she could feel the temperature in the house cooling without any heat coming from the furnace. An entire night without heat could freeze the pipes. The pipes could burst. The place could flood.

Not a good thing.

So it was going to have to be the lesser of two evils and that was Cam Pratt.

Eden sighed and grumbled some more.

But in the end she resigned herself to having to ask for help.

From the monster she'd created.

Chapter Three

Before she could force herself to go next door and ask for Cam Pratt's help with her electrical outage, Eden decided that if she was going to have to be seen, she had to make sure she wasn't too unsightly.

After returning home from the police station she'd put on a pair of flannel pajama pants and a long-sleeved thermal-knit T-shirt so she'd be comfortable to work around the house. Since the clothes weren't revealing, she decided not to change back into what she'd been wearing that afternoon.

But when it came to her face and hair? If she'd been about to meet up with anyone other than Cam Pratt she probably would have gone as she was—face scrubbed clean, hair stuck in an untidy ponytail.

Only she wasn't meeting up with anyone else and she just couldn't go without reapplying blush and mascara using her purse compact and the glow of the moon coming through her bedroom window.

Hating herself for her vanity, she also took her hair down from the ponytail, brushed it, and then pulled it to her crown once again, this time holding it with a clip rather than a plain rubber band.

Nothing fancy, she judged upon final inspection in the compact mirror, but passable.

Still dreading seeing Cam again today, she nevertheless resigned herself to it, slipped on a peacoat and felt her way to the front door to go out into the cold night, regretting that she'd put this off now that it occurred to her that it was after ten o'clock and he might have gone to bed.

If he had she was just going to freeze to death, she decided. Better that than waking him up.

He hadn't gone to bed, though. Because once Eden had crossed their joined-at-the-property-line driveways and was walking in front of his house, she could see that not only were his lights still on, he was in his living room. In fact, he was in clear view through the undraped picture window as she climbed the four steps to his front porch.

He'd apparently showered in the time between her ogling him and now. He was dressed in a different pair of sweatpants—gray ones—and another white T-shirt that had long sleeves instead of short. Although the T-shirt didn't cling to him with the dampness of perspiration, it did fit him tightly enough to prove the chin-ups had been worth it because the knit followed his shoulders, biceps and the expanse of his chest to great effect.

Really great effect…

Inside he was drying his hair with a towel in one hand

while using the other to hold the TV listings he was scanning. He didn't notice Eden's approach and, once again, she couldn't refrain from covertly watching him.

It would have been helpful if the good-looking teenage boy hadn't grown up to be one of the hottest men she'd ever seen. And while it *shouldn't* have had any effect on her, it did.

"I'm just tired," she whispered to herself again.

He'd finished drying his hair and he draped the towel over one shoulder. But running his hands through that wavy hair, finger-combing it back on top, didn't bolster her resistance because even that haphazard grooming gave him a sexiness that was so potent it came through the glass of the picture window and nearly knocked Eden's socks off.

Before she could lapse into another transfixed state, she forced herself to march the rest of the distance to his door and ring the bell.

She also made sure to stare straight ahead so she didn't give any indication that she even knew he was right there in his living room, and as a result she only saw him from the corner of her eye when he peered out the window to see who she was.

Her enthusiasm for being there was not boosted by the epithet she heard him say when he saw her. But she stood her ground, bracing for more of his unpleasantness when he opened the door.

"I'm sorry to bother you," she said before he made it any more clear how he felt about her being there. "But I knocked out my power, I don't know where the breaker box is and I can't find my flashlight. I thought, since the houses are alike, you might—"

"Know where the box is and have a flashlight," he finished for her. Sardonically and impatiently, of course.

This was getting old.

"Yes," she said.

She half expected him to refuse. But after a moment of glaring at her yet again he pushed open his screen door and stepped aside, inviting her in.

"Thanks," she muttered.

"I'll put on some shoes and get a coat. I'll have to show you where the box is," he said begrudgingly, leaving her standing in the entry as he went the six feet to the hallway that led to the bedrooms in her house, too, and disappeared around the corner.

Eden didn't make herself at home but she did peer from where she was into his living room.

Decorating was not his long suit.

The room was furnished for comfort not for style. There was a large brown leather sofa and matching armchair beside each other, both of them facing the television rather than angled to allow for conversation. In front of the sofa was a coffee table cluttered with what appeared to be the remnants of Cam's dinner and a few meals before it. But other than a serviceable end table between the couch and chair, one lamp, and a television and stereo system all together on an elaborate entertainment center, there wasn't a single knickknack or picture on the wall. There also wasn't one book on the built-in bookshelves and Eden marveled at that fact, thinking that her moving expenses would have been considerably less had she not had boxes and boxes and boxes of books.

"I'd think it would occur to a brain trust like you to

ask where something like the breaker box is in a house you'd just bought."

He's ba-ack....

Eden turned her head from the direction of the living room, glancing at him again as he rejoined her in the entry wearing running shoes and a gray hooded sweatshirt, and carrying a flashlight the size of a drainpipe.

"You just aren't going to let up, are you?" she said, more to herself than to him.

"Let up on what?" he asked, pretending not to know what she was referring to.

And that was when Eden decided that they were never going to be able to merely go on from here. That awkward or not, she needed to address the events that had put this thorn in his side and apologize to him if she ever hoped for him to treat her civilly.

"I know I was awful to you when our mothers arranged for me to tutor you in physics—"

"*Awful?* You spent every session calling me stupid, calling me every other lousy name you could come up with to let me know you thought I was too ignorant to live. I'd say *brutal* is more what you were to me," he said as if she'd unleashed something in him.

Eden hid her grimace by dropping her head and rubbing her forehead. "Okay, brutal," she conceded, embarrassed and wishing he didn't recall quite so much.

"You said you were amazed an ignoramus like me could even read," he continued. "That I had no business in a kindergarten class, let alone a physics class. You asked me if you were going to get honorable mention at the bottom of my diploma because I wasn't able to get it on my own. You—"

"I remember it all," Eden said to keep him from going on, shoring up her courage to look at him again. "It's the one thing that I'm mortified I did. I'd never treated anyone that way before and I never have since."

"Am I supposed to feel *special* to have been singled out?" he asked.

"No. But it *was* special circumstances. And it wasn't the real me and I'm sorry."

"Who was it, if it wasn't the *real* you?"

"It was a person who was out of her league being a sixteen-year-old senior. A person who was the target of what passed for humor with you older, cool people every day—*four-eyes, pizza-face, metal-mouth, pump-kinhead, Halloween-hair, geek-bot, nerd-girl—*"

"I don't recall ever calling you any of that. Or even being aware of you until the tutoring."

"But your friends, your crowd, did—Steve Foster, Greg Simmons, Frankie Franklin—they were the worst. They never gave it a rest. Even though I tried to keep to the shadows, I was still fair game that whole year. And then I came home from school one day—a month before I thought it was going to end—and my mother told me I had to tutor you, of all people."

"Because I needed a little help. Kind of like you do right now. But I'll bet you're not thinking of yourself as dumber than dirt, are you? And I didn't need the help because I was too dense to learn the stuff any other way," he said defensively, as if he'd been waiting all these years to get that in. "I'll grant you that I wasn't an A student, but I was average. In everything but physics. Plus I hadn't given it the time I should have when it came to studying. I thought I could take the easy way out. But did you just look at it like that? Not the almighty Eden Perry."

"*Almighty?* That's the last thing I thought I was. I didn't have a drop of self-confidence or self-esteem and I was going to have to be alone, in a room, one-on-one with one of the popular people. I would have rather poked my own eyes out. I was so sure *you* were going to ridicule *me,* that I decided to—" She tried to think of how to temper what she was going to say. But the best she could come up with was, "I decided to cut you off at the knees before you had the chance to do it to me," she finished quietly.

"A preemptive strike?" he said as if he wasn't buying it.

"Yes, a preemptive strike," Eden confirmed anyway. "So I went in and acted as if I thought you were… Well, you know how I acted."

"I was already embarrassed that my mother was making me be tutored. By a girl. A girl who was two years *younger* than I was. But I didn't go in putting you down. And I'd never called you names before, either, so I didn't have that coming."

"I know," she said, a little amazed by just how furious he was.

"And once you saw that I wasn't going to do it to you, why didn't you quit doing it to me?"

Eden made another pained, embarrassed face but this time she didn't hide it. "It was…I don't know…I guess there was some payback in it for everything I went through the rest of the time even though it wasn't you doing it. Plus once I'd started, I was afraid if I stopped I'd really be in for it—from you along with the rest of your clique. And that's sort of how I am, I guess—once I dig in my heels it's hard for me to change course."

"So you kept it up until I felt as lousy as you did?"

Maybe he wasn't *only* furious with her.

She'd assumed from his reaction to her since their paths had crossed again that he just didn't like her. And with good cause. She'd never thought that what she'd done all those years ago might have had more impact than that. Somehow all this time she'd believed that that wasn't possible. Her goads and taunts had been tossed at someone who she'd imagined *couldn't* be hurt. But now she wasn't so sure.

"I didn't think anything I said would actually affect someone like you. I was a nothing and you were king of the high school world. I've hated thinking back on how I spoke to you, but was what I did even worse? Did I…scar you in some way?"

He didn't like that question. He stood a little straighter, his chiseled chin raised a fraction of an inch before he said, "You left a mark but I wouldn't call it a scar."

Eden was concerned that he was lying. That he was covering up just how much she really had injured him, and that thought made what she'd done seem even worse.

"I'm so sorry," she repeated. "I was never proud of what I did—in fact I was so ashamed of it that I've never told a single soul, not even my sisters. But I honestly didn't think it would have any repercussions. I wondered if you'd even remember me today when Luke Walker said you were who I'd be working with." She paused a moment and then in the name of honesty, added, "Or at least I was *hoping* you wouldn't remember me."

Cam didn't say anything. He just let his deep blue eyes bore into her and she couldn't tell what he might be thinking. But she could see now that the same way she still carried the wounds of other people's words, he carried the wounds of hers and that prompted her to repeat a heartfelt, "I am truly sorry. If I could take it back, I would. And honestly, I knew you weren't stupid. It was an awful…" She stumbled over the word he'd already found lacking and amended it to, "—a terrible, terrible thing to do and no one should have known that better than me because I was living it every day myself."

He still didn't say anything for a while and she wondered if her explanation and apology were too little too late. She wouldn't have blamed him if that were the case. Certainly if one of her tormentors were standing there saying the same things to her she didn't think it would make any difference—she still would have disliked them intensely.

But then Cam's expression seemed to soften slightly—only slightly—and he said, "Metal-mouth, four-eyes, pizza-face, Halloween-hair and what else?"

"Pumpkinhead, geek-bot and nerd-girl, just to name a few."

"And I got the brunt of you being called all that?"

"You could think of it as taking one for the team," she suggested carefully, trying a tiny bit of levity to see if he'd respond to it.

And, lo and behold, he did.

He smiled. Only a little. And maybe in spite of himself. But it was a smile nevertheless.

And if he was handsome scowling, it was nothing

compared to how good he looked when that face relaxed with amusement.

"Taking one for the team?" he repeated.

"You could factor in that I really was only a scared, insecure kid—not that I'm excusing my behaviour. And that I *have* regretted it all these years, if that helps any. And really, when all is said and done, can you hate somebody in ducky pants?"

Her second stab at a joke broadened the smile. He glanced down at her pajama pants—brown flannel printed with goofy-looking ducks.

"They're mallards," Cam corrected. "And I suppose I'll think it over while I turn your lights back on."

It wasn't overt forgiveness but at that point, Eden decided to take what she could get.

"Thanks," she said.

Cam nodded toward his front door. "After you."

Eden went out into the cold again and Cam followed her as she retraced her steps, keeping her fingers crossed that peace might really have been reached between them.

The inside of her house was remarkably cooler than the inside of his and Eden knew she'd made the right choice in asking him for help.

Cam took the lead once the front door was closed behind them, using his flashlight to help navigate around and through packing boxes and debris to get to the basement.

Eden followed, happy not to be going down into the blackness of the basement alone.

The circuit box was under the stairs and one flip of the main breaker set music playing upstairs, letting them know it had worked.

."There's a light here," Cam said, pulling a string that turned on a bare bulb under the steps to prove his point.

Eden hadn't realized until that moment how close they were standing. Or in what position. But they were standing very close in the small space beneath the stairs, and he'd pivoted away from the breaker box to face her.

They were so close that she had to look almost straight up at him, the way she might have tipped her head if they were about to kiss.

Which, of course, they weren't.

But once more that strange Cam-trance thing happened and she suddenly found herself staring up into his dark eyes, thinking about what it might be like if he *did* kiss her. If he just leaned down a little and pressed his lips to hers.

Cam Pratt, of all people…

Then it registered that her mind was wandering again and Eden yanked herself out of it, stepping from under the stairs in a hurry.

"I'd better go turn some things off or this is going to trip again," she said as her exit excuse, dashing up the steps far ahead of Cam.

She had turned off the stereo and some of the lights by the time he reached her, and she could hear the heat switching on.

"I really appreciate this," she told him as he headed for the front door.

"I keep one of those lights that work on batteries stuck to the wall next to the breaker box down there so when this happens I have that option, too. In case the flashlight isn't easy to get to for some reason."

"That's a fabulous idea," she said, too effusively because she was overcompensating for calling him stupid all those years ago. She toned it down and added, "Plus I'll be more careful about how many things I have on at once. But you know how it is when you move—I was going from room to room looking for what I needed in all the boxes so every light was on."

He merely nodded. There wasn't anything to say to her ramblings. But he was watching her with those penetrating eyes again as they stood at her door. Eden wasn't sure what else to say, either.

Cam broke the silence—and the meeting of their eyes—by glancing at her pajama pants again.

"Ducky pants, huh?"

"They were my back-to-the-cold-of-Montana present to myself."

He sighed. "Well, I guess you're right, you can't hate somebody in ducky pants."

This time Eden smiled. "Does that mean I've been granted amnesty?"

He didn't answer immediately. Instead he raised his gaze to hers once again and gave her a small, forgiving smile. "Yeah, I suppose it does."

Eden wasn't sure if she'd been carrying around even more guilt than she'd realized or if it had something to do with how bowled over she'd been by this guy from the start, but the relief she felt was like a huge, heavy weight lifted from her shoulders. And she was far more pleased than seemed warranted, too.

But she decided to simply enjoy it and smiled back at him a second time. "Thank you," she said, meaning it.

He merely nodded and opened her door to go.

"And thanks again for help with the breaker box," she called to his back as he walked across her porch.

He didn't turn around, he just raised the hand that held his flashlight and said, "Anytime."

And as Eden closed her door to the sight of that man who had so enthralled her already tonight, she was a little shocked at just how tempting it was to turn on every light in the house, hit the microwave start button the way she had earlier and trip the breaker all over again.

Just so she could take him up on that offer and get him back there.

Cam Pratt.

Of all people.

Chapter Four

"Help has arrived. Bearing coffee and doughnuts."

Eden craned around a stack of boxes in her living room to see her sister Eve come through her front door bright and early the next morning. "I'm saved! I can't find my coffeemaker."

Eve went directly to the kitchen to deposit the cups and doughnut box. Once she had, she turned to Eden, who had followed her, and gave her a hug.

"I'm *so* glad you're back!" Eve said just before she let go of Eden.

"Me, too. Even if these temperatures are a shock to my system after Hawaii," Eden responded.

She took the coffee that was intended for her, curved both hands around the cup to warm them and, after a sip, sat on one of the kitchen chairs at the table.

"How was Billings?" she asked her sister as Eve sat across from her.

"It was fine. I'm sorry I couldn't be here when you got in yesterday. I wanted to be. But the Reverend made an appointment to see his attorney and his headache doctor, and I was the only one of the grandchildren who could take him. And you know you can't go to Billings and not have dinner with the folks and Uncle Carl and Aunt Sheila, and spend the night or everyone gets upset. So I was stuck. But I'm here now and I'm all yours for the whole day. On one condition," Eve added.

They'd each settled on a doughnut and Eden chose to ignore the *on one condition* portion of what her sister had said as she took a bite of hers.

"How are the folks?" she asked after savoring the sweet fried cake.

"Same as always—good," Eve answered. "They told me to say hi and for you to get to Billings to see them as soon as you can."

"I will. And how is the Reverend?" They'd never called their grandfather—who had been Northbridge's reverend until his retirement a few years earlier—anything else. He wasn't a cuddly kind of man and had never invited anything but formality. From anyone, as far as Eden could tell.

"The Reverend's the same, too. The man will die the way he's lived—with a stick up his butt."

Eden laughed at her sister's bluntness. "Why was he seeing his lawyer and a doctor?"

"You know the Reverend—no explanations and I certainly wasn't allowed in on either appointment. I was lucky to get a thanks for taking him everywhere he needed to go."

"Do you think the renewed interest in the bank robbery and Celeste was why he wanted to talk to the lawyer?"

Eve shrugged elaborately as she sipped her coffee and chose a second doughnut.

"And maybe he's stressed-out about it and that's why he's having his headaches again," Eden continued to postulate.

"Hard to say. I can't believe he *isn't* stressed-out by having all this old stuff brought up again. You know that stiff-upper-lip-never-talk-about-it thing he does has to be hiding what he really feels. And having his wife run off with a bank robber? That had to have been the worst, the most humiliating thing that ever happened in his life. But of course he's acting as if he's above it all." Eve took a bite of her doughnut and then said, "He says hello, too, by the way. And that he's looking forward to seeing you again after so long."

Eden wrinkled her nose. It wasn't that she *dis*liked her grandfather, but he wasn't her favorite person, either. She certainly hadn't been sorry that of all her family, he'd never visited her in Hawaii.

"Yeah, I think you might be in for it," Eve said, interpreting Eden's nose wrinkle. "The Reverend doesn't seem particularly happy that you've agreed to do the age progression on Celeste. He said he doesn't see the point in pursuing what's long past and important to no one," Eve finished, mimicking their grandfather's stiff speech pattern.

"It's important to a whole lot of authorities," Eden said. "Important enough that if I didn't do it they'd get someone else to."

"I'm just warning you." Eve brushed crumbs off her hands.

"I guess it's good to go in knowing what I'll have coming but it doesn't make me want to see him more."

Eve took a turn ignoring what Eden had said and changed the subject. "Now for my one condition as payment for my help. I want you to be my plus-one at Luke Walker's wedding tonight."

"Your love life is in sorry shape if I have to be your plus-one," Eden said with a laugh.

"There's no question that my love life is in sorry shape. But I *want* you to be my plus-one. I thought it would be a good opportunity for you to jump right into things again here. See some people, get reacquainted. The Walkers would have invited you themselves if they had known you would be here."

"Why are they having a wedding on a Tuesday night?"

"The minister they wanted to perform the ceremony is an old friend of the bride and this was the only time he could get here."

"But still, I have this whole house to put together," Eden demurred.

"We'll work all day and then stop, get pretty and go to the wedding. I'm not letting you hibernate. You've been doing that since Alika died and now you're here and starting over and you need to do it right. Faith is coming in next week and I swear that I'm going to get you both going again if it's the last thing I ever do."

"Like a couple of stalled engines?" Eden asked, laughing again.

"Like a couple of cars that have been up on blocks. It was good that Faith spent all that time with you in

Hawaii after her divorce but I know you both just used it to hide out from life together. Faith doesn't know what to do with herself and you've thrown yourself into work since Alika died. But things have to change and now's the time for it."

"And you think that starts with my going to a wedding tonight."

"It's as good a place as any. So I RSVP'd for me and my plus-one and you're it."

Eve was right that Eden had thrown herself into work as a kind of protective shell to get through the last awful year and she had made up her mind to put some effort into coming out of that shell when she'd decided to move back to Northbridge. Eve was probably also right that tonight, at a wedding, was as good a place as any to start.

"Okay," she said as if she were conceding reluctantly when, in fact, she wasn't. "But we'd better get a whole lot of stuff done today to make up for losing tonight."

"We will," Eve assured. "I told you, I'm all yours."

But neither of them was in enough of a hurry to leave the coffee they were still drinking.

Eve's attention did seem to turn to the job at hand, though, when she glanced around at the mess. "The house is okay?" she said.

Eve had done Eden's house hunting for her and served as her proxy at the closing.

"It's just the way I remembered it. Unfortunately I never had occasion to find out where the circuit box is when I babysat here for the Dundees," Eden said, going on to tell her sister about the blackout of previous evening.

"And speaking of Cam Pratt," Eden said when she'd

finished with the entire story. "You didn't tell me he lived next door."

"Why? Does it matter?"

Eden couldn't very well say it did when Eve didn't know what had gone on with Cam years ago, so she said, "No, it just might have been nice to know. The Realtor led me to believe my neighbors would be people named Poppazitto."

"They own the place but Cam lives there and is probably going to buy it."

"So I've heard."

Eve finished her coffee and took the cup to the trash bag in the corner. "Cam's a good guy," she said along the way. "He helped you last night, didn't he?"

"Uh-huh," Eden said noncommittally, thinking that he'd helped her out of a whole lot of rest the night before. She hadn't been able to stop the image of him from haunting her each time she'd closed her eyes and for some reason it had made her too restless to fall asleep.

"I'll bet he was surprised to see how you'd changed from when you used to tutor him," Eve said, laughing at the thought.

"He didn't seem to be."

"How could he *not* have been? You're so different you don't look like the same person—that's another reason I want you to go tonight, I want to be there when everyone sees you now."

"Very few thirty-one-year-old people look exactly like they did when they were sixteen. Even Cam has changed," Eden said, picturing him again in her mind and once more judging the changes to be improvements.

She didn't have any idea what alerted her sister to her

thoughts, but apparently something did because Eve's eyebrows rose. "Do you have a little thing for Cam?"

"Don't be silly. Of course I don't," Eden said, hoping it came out as even-toned as she'd wanted it to so she didn't raise any more suspicions in her sister's mind.

But whether it had or not, Eve was still not convinced. "Did you have a secret crush on him when you tutored him?" she said as if she'd just hit on a surprise of her own. "He *was* the big man on campus, as I recall. And you were the mousy kid who should have been a sophomore rather than a senior, who got to be all alone with him to teach him… What was it?"

"Physics," Eden said, rolling her eyes at the fiction her sister was weaving. "And no, I absolutely didn't have a crush on him, secret or not. I didn't even like him."

"Then maybe you just like him now," Eve said, switching gears.

"Or maybe I was just saying I thought I was going to be living next door to people named Poppazitto and I'm not," Eden said, taking her own cup to the trash.

But again Eve didn't seem to be fooled because when Eden turned back to her, Eve was grinning. "Cam will be there tonight, you know? Luke Walker is marrying Cam's half sister."

"Cam has a half sister?" Eden asked, interested in this bit of news but also hoping it would distract Eve.

"That's right, you don't know the dirt, do you?" Eve said. "Well, Cam's father had two daughters with the woman he left Cam's mother for. One of them was a nightmare and she ended up dead when the meth lab she was living in exploded. But Karis—the other Pratt half sister—is nice and she came here with her sister's baby, thinking Luke might be the baby's father because he'd been married to her sister for a while. It turned out that he *isn't* the baby's father, but that's how Luke and Karis got together and now Luke and Karis are adopting the baby and getting married tonight."

If that story wasn't a distraction, Eden didn't know what was.

But it wasn't distraction enough because Eve managed to go full circle and ended with, "So Cam will be there tonight and you'll get to see him again."

"I don't care about seeing him," Eden insisted, lying through her teeth when the truth was, she'd been looking out every window she passed since she got up this morning, hoping to catch sight of him. And failing. And being inexplicably disappointed each time.

"I don't kno-oh," Eve said, making two syllables and a song out of *know.* "I think there's more going on here than you want to tell and I'll bet it's an old crush."

Eden rolled her eyes again, shook her head and said, "If only you knew how wrong you are."

At least about there being an old crush.

But a new crush?

Well, maybe not exactly a *crush.*

But as much as Eden hated to admit it even to herself, deep down there might be brewing the tiniest hint of something a little like that.

The wedding of Luke Walker and Karis Pratt was held at the Pratt family home. The large house had been built by the Pratt's maternal great-grandfather, and was where the first seven Pratt siblings had all grown up.

The ceremony was short, sweet and traditional, with

the bride beautiful in a white suit composed of a fitted jacket and skirt, and the groom handsome in a navy-blue suit of his own.

But not as handsome as Cam—that was what Eden thought as her gaze drifted to him from the moment he stepped up as one of the groomsmen. He and Luke's brothers—who were also groomsmen—wore blue suits, as well. And despite the fact that the Walker men were indisputably a good-looking lot, to Eden, Cam had them all beat by a mile.

Which was not something she *wanted* to think.

But she just couldn't help it. Any more than she could take her eyes off him from the wedding's very beginning to the pronouncement of man and wife, and the kiss.

The kiss that made her recall her own thoughts about what it might have been like to kiss Cam the night before.

A recollection she shunned the minute she realized she was having it.

When the ceremony was over, congratulations were given during an informal receiving line. Then champagne began to flow, and an elaborate buffet of food and a three-tiered cake were unveiled.

After a full day of making headway putting her new house in order, Eden had showered and shampooed her hair, and slipped into a dress she'd worn to the last wedding she'd attended. It was a fairly simple, knee-length silk halter dress in an exotic print of black, brown and beige. The dress wasn't tight but it did follow her curves nicely and bare her shoulders.

On her feet she wore her sassy and very pointy black

satin mules with the jeweled flowers, golden rope cutouts and thin three-inch heels.

She'd scrunched her damp hair just enough to give it a little added fullness without frizz, added a taupe-colored eye shadow to her blush and mascara regimen, and as a finishing touch she'd slipped several hoop bracelets over one wrist.

All together she'd been pleased with how she'd looked and had left home feeling comfortable and confident.

That had been reinforced at the Pratt house where old friends and acquaintances marveled at the changes in her. But although she didn't understand it, she discovered as the evening wore on that the approval—and maybe admiration—of only one person was what she craved. And that person didn't come anywhere near her.

Maybe things with Cam weren't as improved as they'd seemed the night before, she fretted as the post-receiving-line mingling got underway and Cam kept his distance. Or maybe she had read more into the night before than had actually existed. Maybe having granted her amnesty still didn't mean that they were going to be friendly. Maybe the best that amnesty afforded her was a cease-fire and she should just be glad for that because that was really what was important in order for them to coexist in the small town.

But still, each time their glances met and he only nodded or raised a chin at her, she wished for more.

Why that should be the case, she didn't know. And what more she wanted from him, she also didn't know. She just wanted more.

She wanted it so much that it was alarming and it took the fun out of the occasion for her.

In fact, she was feeling so disheartened as she turned from the buffet table with a slice of wedding cake, that rather than joining any of the other guests who were chatting while they ate theirs, she went to the entryway and sat alone, one step up from the bottom.

And that was when Cam chose to seek her out. One bite into the cake and there he was, sitting next to her.

"Tired of talking?" he asked in greeting.

"No, not at all," she answered with a tinge more eagerness than she would have liked. But she was worried that now that he'd finally approached her, he might leave her to solitude if she didn't convince him otherwise. Then, as an excuse for exiling herself, she added, "Pointy shoes. I needed to sit for a minute."

"Ah," he said, in acknowledgment.

That left a lull Eden didn't know how to fill because her mind suddenly went blank.

"So are the lights still on at your place?" he asked.

Okay, not a great conversation starter but it was more than she'd been able to come up with.

"They are, thanks," she said. "And you'll be happy to know that I found my flashlight today, too. Just in case."

Ugh. She knew she wasn't helping matters. But she just couldn't get her brain to function.

Which was why all she could think to say next was, "Nice wedding."

"I thought so, too."

"Eve told me Karis is your half sister."

"Mmm-hmm. There were two of them but the other one died."

"That's what Eve said. It looks as if Karis fits in, though. She seems like one of the family."

"Yeah, we all think of her that way now. Even me," he added in a bit of an aside that drew Eden's glance from the bride in the distance to Cam.

"Even you?"

"I wasn't too sure about Karis when she first showed up. Her sister had come around before that and Lea was trouble. Plus I guess I learned not to be too trusting working in Detroit. But Karis won me over."

"Detroit?" Eden said, pleased to have something to build on. "Don't tell me you put a branch of your family's dry cleaning business there."

"No, we all left the dry cleaning business to Mara to run here in Northbridge. I was a cop in the heart of Detroit."

"Really? How did you get there, doing that?" she asked as if this was the first she'd heard of it when, in fact, Luke Walker had told her that the day before at the police station.

He shrugged one shoulder. "I left home to go to college—" He paused and there was challenge in the arch of his right eyebrow. "Did you want to make a crack about how surprised you are that I went to college?"

"No," she said, chastising him with her tone for even thinking that. "Did you go to college in Detroit?"

"Uh-uh. From here I went to Mesa College, in Grand Junction, Colorado. I finished with a degree in business administration, didn't know what I wanted to do, so I joined the army."

"You did?" she said.

"That surprises you?"

She could tell he was still on the verge of taking offense and she chose her words carefully. "Yes, a little. You said you hated anything inflexible—like physics. I guess I wouldn't have thought you would volunteer for something so regimented."

"I may have exaggerated when it came to physics to sound cool," he said with a mischievous grin. "Anyway, I was an MP—military police—"

Eden smiled. "I know what an MP is."

He answered her smile with one of his own. "Just wanted to be clear," he said and she realized he'd been teasing her. Then he continued, "Anyway, I liked being a cop and when I got out of the service some other things led me to Detroit and I got on the force there."

Some other things led him to Detroit....

Apparently he didn't want to say what those other things were—which would have answered her question about why he'd ended up in Detroit.

But Eden thought that this new relationship they were forming was too tenuous to push for what he wasn't willing to disclose, so she pretended not to notice and said, "How long were you a cop in Detroit?"

"Four years."

"And then you came back here to be a cop?"

"I did something else there for a little while. Six months. Then I came back here."

He also didn't seem to want to get into any details about what else he'd done for those six months and again she thought it unwise to pry. So instead she said, "And can you be a *trusting* cop here?"

Something about that made him smile and she liked the way it looked a little too much. "Things here are pretty straightforward. But when Karis came around after her sister had conned us out of money, she took some heat from me. It all worked out, though, and you're right—she has become one of the family. And she deserves a nice wedding."

That neatly tied up what had launched this conversation but he'd left her with more questions than she'd started with and Eden wasn't sure where to go from there.

Cam took the lead again, however, and said, "What about you? Hawaii?" he asked, as if it were the moon.

Eden nodded and took her cue from him to talk about her path out of and back to Northbridge. "I went from here to college in Philadelphia. I thought I wanted to be a doctor so I was taking biology and anatomy courses with art as my elective. There was one other person— a guy—who was taking the same combination of anatomy and art and we became friends. He wanted to be a forensic sculptor and the more he talked about it the more interested I became in forensic art, too. That was how I got into this line of work."

"And Hawaii?"

"Forensic art is a freelance business. I traveled all over doing it. A case took me to Hawaii and—" She decided she wasn't at a stage herself where she wanted to get into anything too personal, so she opted to omit details of her own. "—I ended up moving there as my home base."

"But now you're back and getting out of the forensic art game," he said, obviously fishing.

"It was time for a change all the way around. I'm ready for small town life again and being close to family."

"Rumor has it that you never even came to visit," he said.

"I never came to Northbridge, no. I'm sure you know that my folks and my aunt and uncle took over a freight business in Billings just after I left for college and moved there. So when I've visited, it's been to Billings. My sisters and cousins would meet me there rather than me coming here. Or everybody would come to see me in Hawaii. When you live in paradise and for no more than the price of a plane ticket your family can spend weeks at a time visiting, you get a lot of company."

He smiled once more. "I'll bet."

"So it isn't as if I haven't been close to my family all this time. But now I want to close the mileage gap, too."

"But still no more forensic art after this age progression on Celeste?"

Eden shook her head. "I'm contracted to do the illustrations for a series of children's book a friend has just sold for publication. At this point painting fairies with peanut butter on their wings has more appeal. So as soon as I finish your job and get the house situated, that's my new career."

They hit another lull and Eden realized she hadn't had any more of her cake since Cam had come on the scene so she took a bite and then said, "This is good, you should have a piece."

"Cut me a chunk of yours and I'll eat it with my fingers."

"Who says I want to share?" she countered even as she did as she'd been told.

He took the confection from the end of her fork when she held it up to him.

Eden watched his long, thick fingers in action, unwillingly picturing that same big hand wielding the towel to dry his hair the previous night and feeling a flutter like butterfly wings in her stomach.

And the flutters weren't halted by the sight of him putting the cake into his mouth—something that she'd never found sexy before and yet now somehow did.

Maybe this is some kind of sudden reawakening, she thought. Maybe grief had put her awareness of the opposite sex and of all things arousing in a coma for the last year and now, out of nowhere, she was just emerging from it. And maybe that reawakening made her supersensitive to the smallest, most inconsequential things. About the first man who happened to cross her path. Not about Cam Pratt in particular, but just about any man.

Although no other men—and there was no shortage of good-looking ones at the wedding—had caused it.

But she didn't want to analyze her feelings too closely because she needed a reason that didn't indicate an attraction to him to explain being turned-on by watching him eat cake with his fingers.

"You're right, this is good cake," he judged when he'd finished his portion.

Eden had taken a forkful of her own to buy herself some time to think of what to talk about next. She was spared when Eve came from the living room into the entry.

"Do you still want me to be the clock-watcher? Because if you do, I'm here to tell you it's eleven," she said to Eden after exchanging a few pleasantries with Cam.

Eden cast him a glance and explained. "I told her to keep an eye on the time and make sure I didn't stay past eleven. I've been up since before dawn working on the house and I thought you'd probably want to get an early start tomorrow on the age progression, so I need some sleep."

"I do want to get an early start tomorrow," he confirmed. "And I should get going, too, for the same reason." Then something seemed to occur to him and, to Eve, he said, "I saw that you drove tonight, Eve, but you shouldn't have to leave because we do. Or go in the opposite direction to take Eden home when we're basically going to the same place. Why don't you stay and enjoy the party and Eden can ride with me?"

Eden was taken aback by his offer. And instantly flooded with a mixture of elation and nervousness and excitement and dread and more contradictory things than she could put her finger on.

Eve glanced at Eden. "Is that all right with you?"

What could she say? That she was feeling so many things that she didn't know if it was a good idea or a bad one?

So she said, "Sure. Fine. Cam's right, then you can stay."

"I'm ready to go, too, so it isn't as if you'll be rushing me out," Eve assured.

To complicate Eden's confusion, the thought of returning to the original plan of her sister driving her home sent a wave of disappointment through her. And before she even knew she was going to speak, she heard herself say, "But still I might as well ride with Cam and save you the trip."

"Okay," Eve agreed, and Eden knew her sister didn't have a clue what a big deal this was.

"I'll get our coats. Do you have one, Cam?" Eve asked then.

"No, I came as-is," Cam answered.

"Is that okay? That I ride with you even if Eve is

leaving, too?" Eden asked him as her sister went to the closet under the stairs where guest coats had been hung.

"I wouldn't have offered if I didn't want to do it," he said in a quiet voice, as though his words were intended for her alone.

Or was she imagining that? Because really, why would there be any intimacy in the way he spoke to her?

Eve reappeared with coats, and Cam and Eden stood.

They all went to say one last congratulations and good-night to the bride and groom, and then they walked out together, parting at the curb to go their separate ways.

When Eden and Cam arrived at his black SUV he opened the door for her and waited for her to get in before closing it and going around the rear to the driver's side.

The inside of his car smelled the way he did—of a fresh-scented soap—and Eden couldn't keep herself from taking a deep breath and savoring it for the moment it took him to get behind the wheel.

She wasn't sure why something popped into her head then to say to him, she was just grateful that it did.

"Are Luke and Karis having a honeymoon?"

"Not much of one," Cam said as he headed away from the Pratt house. "They're taking the baby and driving to Denver to tie up some loose ends Karis left there. It's time off work, but I don't know if I'd call it a honeymoon. They're so happy I guess it seems like one to them."

"Lucky them," Eden said softly, fighting a twinge of envy and nostalgia brought on by the memory of having once felt that way herself.

"Yeah, lucky them," Cam agreed almost as softly, and

unless Eden was mistaken, also with a note of envy and nostalgia in his tone.

Neither of them said anything else the rest of the brief drive home but the silence didn't make Eden uncomfortable. It was almost as if it was called for—a moment of silence to mourn something she'd lost. And maybe something he had, too.

Then he was pulling into his driveway, going all the way back to park in his garage where they both got out.

"I'd better walk over with you and make sure you have lights to get in," Cam said as they met at the rear of his SUV.

"You don't have to do that. Without me there to abuse it I'm sure the power hasn't blown," Eden demurred, even though she liked that he just fell into step beside her as she went to the rear of her house.

When they reached the door, she unlocked it, then opened it and flipped on the lights without going inside.

"What did I tell you? No problem," Eden said as the golden glow flooded out.

"Glad to see it."

"So what time tomorrow?" she asked then, turning to face him.

"I have to be in at seven but I'll need to do my beginning-of-shift things so it'd be a waste of your time to come that early. Maybe eight-thirty or so? Or I can just expect you when I see you."

This was a very big change from the way he'd behaved the day before and Eden appreciated it.

"I'll shoot for eight-thirty," she told him.

"Great."

She assumed he would just leave then. But he didn't.

And he didn't seem aware of the fact that he probably should have. Instead he looked as if he were lost in his own thoughts, in staring down into her eyes.

Once more the end of the previous night came into Eden's mind and again she recalled that she had wondered then what it might have been like if he kissed her. Was that what he was thinking about tonight?

And what if he was? she asked herself. What if, any minute now, he leaned in just a little, bent over just a little, and kissed her? Just a little...

No man had kissed her in a year.

No man except Alika had kissed her in many years.

What would she do?

She wasn't sure.

But maybe she'd like to find out....

She tipped her chin upward. She looked at Cam's mouth.

She saw him do a bit of that leaning in, of that bending over...

He's going to kiss me....

Cam Pratt is going to kiss me....

Her heart beat faster.

Those flutters in her stomach began again.

A nervous tingle danced across the surface of her skin.

She wanted him to kiss her....

But he didn't.

As if something had snapped him out of whatever had brought him that far, he stood straighter and said, "See you in the morning."

Slightly dumbstruck, Eden nodded, hoping that if she'd been wrong, if he *hadn't* been about to kiss her, he didn't have any idea what she'd been thinking. Wanting.

"See you in the morning," she repeated, telling herself it was better that he *hadn't* kissed her. Trying to make herself believe it.

Then, as an afterthought as he started off in the direction of his house she added, "Thanks for the ride home."

"Sure," he called back.

His voice had a kind of cragginess to it. Was that because *not* kissing her had been rough on him?

She hoped so.

It would serve him right.

Because standing there unkissed when she'd been so ready to be kissed was definitely rough on her.

Chapter Five

"I didn't think you'd need so much stuff."

Eden glanced up from the computer screen. Cam was standing in the doorway of the small room at the police station. It was after ten on Wednesday morning and she'd been setting up since her arrival at 8:30 when the woman who acted as dispatcher and office manager had handed Eden a note from him.

"Did you get the bull out of the road?" she asked in lieu of a greeting of her own, referring to the reason he'd given in his note for why he hadn't been there.

"The O'Murray's bull," he said. "It was in the middle of the old north road, charging cars."

"So they called you? Were you a matador in Detroit?" she joked, swiveling in her seat to face him and taking in the sight of his dark blue uniform shirt and jeans. And wishing she could have judged him something less than fabulous-looking with his handsome face clean-shaven and his wavy hair slightly mussed from the outdoors.

"We could have used a matador but that's hardly me. This job just covers everything, including bull wrangling. It took O'Murray, his wife, his two sons, the fire department and me to get that dumb bull out of the road. But not before it had butted a dent in the side panel of O'Murray's truck. I thought we were going to have to call the vet to tranquilize it."

"The bull or the truck?"

He laughed. "The bull."

Cam came to stand beside her then. In order to survey all she had set out on the tabletop to the right of the computer, he leaned slightly over it. Just enough so that his rear end jutted out. At Eden's eye level. And she couldn't help looking before she even realized what she was doing.

Looking and thinking, *bang-up butt...*

"Are you putting a family album together while you wait for me or what?"

The sound of his voice snapped her out of staring at his tight, perfectly shaped rump and forced her to pay attention to what he was asking as he glanced from one photograph to another.

"A family album? No, not quite..." Her voice came out like a squeaky little girl's. She had to clear her throat to go on.

"Frog," she said to explain her vocal deficiency. Then, as if it really had only been a frog in her throat and not a constriction caused by ogling his very, very fine derriere, she said, "I thought you knew something about this process and that's why you were assigned this duty."

"I was assigned this duty because I've been involved with cases that used age progressions and facial reconstruction to help identify victims or locate missing children. But the *process* was already a thing of the past when I got involved. My part was just a matter of showing the finished product around to see if anyone recognized the person in the picture—usually in conjunction with whatever detectives were on the case. That's still more than anyone around here has had to do with this kind of thing, so here I am," he explained.

"Then you don't know anything about how the end product gets to be."

"No more than the next guy."

"Okay, I'll give you the quick course. I need pictures of everyone who's related to Celeste so I can compile and piece together likenesses we may share with her, and aging similarities—"

"But you're all young. How is the way you're aging at a minute-past-thirty going to tell us how she might look in her seventies?"

"Well, for instance," Eden said, standing and putting her focus on the job at hand by looking at what he was looking at rather than at him. "See this crease just below the eyes of all of the grandchildren—me, included?" She pointed out what she was referring to in several of the photographs.

Cam picked up a few of them to have an even closer look, straightening again.

"I can hardly make that out," he said of the under-eye crease after studying the pictures. "I would never have noticed it on my own."

"Probably because it doesn't really matter to what

you do. But noticing the tiniest details of faces is part of what I do." The way she kept noticing the details of his face—like the lines that went from the sides of his nose to the corners of that mouth she'd wanted to kiss the night before....

"Anyway," she continued, "the Reverend doesn't have that crease, so I'm gambling on it being something we all inherited from Celeste. Something she could have, too."

"But you could have inherited it from someone else, from another relative generations before on the Reverend's side."

"That's true. But as long as there's the possibility that it's a trait we share with Celeste, I can factor it in. And see how it's more shallow in our younger pictures, and deepening as each of us gets older? As I age the image of Celeste, I'll give her that under-the-eye line and make it more pronounced, add some sag and probably a little puffiness. That contributes to the potential for the overall image to be more accurate. Although it won't be as accurate as a three-dimensional one would be."

"Really?" Cam said, sounding interested as he continued to study the pictures. "A three-dimensional image, as in a sculpture?"

"Right."

"I thought computers could do everything better than we can."

He was standing very close beside her and the scent of fresh air and soap wafted toward her. It couldn't have smelled better if it had been a high-priced men's cologne. But she tried not to let it affect her.

"The best end products come when I can build from

an actual skull—" She saw him grimace. "I know, gory and gross."

"I only encountered one in the course of my big-city career and it was definitely gory and gross. I can't say I was sorry to leave it to the coroner to handle. But that's what you *prefer?*"

"Only because it gives the best basis to begin with. Believe me, what I *prefer* now is getting out of this work completely, which is why I am."

His gaze went from the photographs to her. "It's gotten to you," he said as if he hadn't thought that when they'd talked about her job before.

Eden shrugged one shoulder. "Yes, it's gotten to me," she admitted. "The job and every connection with the criminal element. I've just…I've had enough."

Since she didn't want to expand any further, she backtracked. "But whether I work from a skull or from pictures, a sculpture will still give a more realistic de-piction than a computer-generated image. It's just that it takes me about a month to do a sculpture and the powers-that-be in this case didn't want to wait even longer or go to that extent."

"What about all the files and old reports? What good will they do you?" Cam asked then, nodding at the storage boxes.

"I doubt if they'll do much, but I also need to know everything I can about what Celeste's habits might have been, if there's any indication that they changed and how. I know her life with the Reverend was pretty austere, but that she'd cut loose with Rider and Dorian before the robbery, that she'd been hanging out at the bar with them, drinking. It would be good to know if she kept that up, if there's any mention of her becoming a heavy drinker. Or a smoker—both of those age the skin prematurely and can cause other alterations in the face—"

"Like a bulbous nose if she broke out of the Reverend's strict policy on sobriety."

"Exactly. Basically I just have to get as much of a feel for her as I can. Then I put it all together and add my own judgment, my own instinct to the mix, and just hope what I come up with is an image that looks enough like her to ring a bell with someone."

"And don't forget we have the description of a possible Celeste from the woman in Bozeman. That should help, shouldn't it?"

"Everything helps—maybe the woman in Bozeman will have remembered that the other waitress she worked with was having trouble seeing to write down her lunch orders and I can do one printout with glasses. Or at the very least, if the waitress in Bozeman *was* Celeste, hearing what she looked like a few years after she left Northbridge can give us an idea of the direction of the changes she was making—in her hair, her clothes, her makeup—"

"The Bozeman description has the hair a darker blond than Celeste's original pale blond, and it wasn't in that braids-coiled-over-the-ears-like-cinnamon-rolls style she'd worn here. It was short. But the Bozeman witness didn't remember whether or not the other waitress was wearing makeup and your grandfather says he wouldn't allow Celeste to."

"So if the waitress in Bozeman *was* my grandmother, we know she'd cut her hair and since most women don't keep it long as they age anyway—we'll use that. As I said, everything helps."

"And where do we begin?"

"I need to go over all the family pictures with a magnifying glass. You can start to read the files and pay special attention to anything that refers to Celeste even if it didn't seem important on the first run-through."

"It's gonna be a long day, isn't it?"

"And into tonight. But if we stick with it we might be able to have pictures you can show around by tomorrow."

Then something else occurred to Eden. "Unless you don't want to drag it out past your shift and you'd rather we work tomorrow, too." In order to have tonight off and maybe spend it with someone he was seeing…

"Nah, we need this done," he said without hesitation. "Let's go straight through."

"No plans for this evening?" She knew she had no business asking that. But it had suddenly struck her that he could be in the middle of a torrid love affair and she just didn't know it. That maybe that was the reason he hadn't kissed her the night before. That maybe the woman he was involved with was simply out of town for a few days and that that was why he'd been solo at his half-sister's wedding and the rest of the time Eden had been in town—

"No, no plans," he answered, interrupting her thoughts. He replaced the photographs on the table without giving any sign that he was aware that she was scavenging for information.

But his answer didn't satisfy her. What if his girlfriend just wasn't back in town yet? Or maybe she lived somewhere else and they only got together on weekends, Eden thought.

"Not even a date with the woman of the moment?"

she heard herself persist in spite of the fact that she was trying to keep herself from doing it.

"No date with the woman of the moment because there isn't any woman of the moment."

Relief. Pure and simple and sweet. For something that shouldn't have made any difference to her in the first place.

I've gone out of my mind....

She'd also made one inquiry too many because Cam stopped being more interested in organizing the file boxes than in her interrogation and looked at her again.

Only now there was a small smile lifting one corner of his sexy mouth.

"Were you just trying to find out if I'm spoken for?"

"Why would I care if you're spoken for?" she countered defensively, hearing the long-ago teenager in her putting him down.

Cam sobered and she knew he'd heard the same thing. She also realized—now that it was too late—that there had been a hint of flirting in his tone.

She couldn't think of a way to rectify what she'd just done without giving herself away and letting him know that attempting to find out if he was spoken for was precisely what she'd been doing.

But she had to try. So she said, "I'm sorry, I don't know why I bit your head off like that. I was only wondering if I was infringing on time you might have planned to spend with someone. A girlfriend or a fiancée or a significant other or someone." The truth, but tempered. She hoped it would fool him and bail her out of that last unintentional skip backward in time.

"Like I said, there's no one," he said much more stiffly than he had a moment before.

"There isn't for me, either," she confessed, not by design, giving herself away after all, and somehow managing to make things better because his expression softened again.

And in a voice almost as quiet as hers had been, he said, "Good to know.

Then he took the magnifying glass that was near the computer's keyboard and handed it to her.

"Let's get to work," he suggested.

Grateful that his old grudge didn't seem renewed, Eden nodded and agreed.

But she still could have kicked herself for that lapse that reminded them both of what she'd hoped they could forget.

Eden had been right—she and Cam worked all day and well into the night before she felt she'd covered all the bases for the computer age progression of Celeste Perry.

They'd eaten lunch at the computer and skipped dinner so when it came time to do the printout it was 11:45 p.m., they were both starving, and the local pizzeria—their sole option for takeout—was closing at midnight.

To get food before it was too late, Cam went for pizza while Eden did the actual printout, and they agreed to meet at her house to eat and look over the culmination of their day's work.

Cam hadn't arrived with the food yet when Eden got home but she knew he'd be there too soon after her own arrival to give her the chance to change out of the pin-striped slacks and sweater set she'd put on early that morning. But she did head for the bathroom to take her hair down from the clip that held it at her crown so she could run a brush through it. She also refreshed her blush and added lip gloss before rushing to the kitchen to remove the two packing boxes from the table and set it with paper plates, cups and napkins.

She'd barely accomplished that when the doorbell rang.

"Pizza delivery," Cam announced when she opened the front door. "I hope ours isn't cold. I had to drop one off to the Jordans down the street on the way."

Eden laughed as she let him in. "You delivered someone's pizza?"

"Stewart—over at the pizzeria—said he didn't need the police to protect him but he did need a service. He needed me to deliver the Jordans' pizza so he could go straight home."

"Cop, matador and pizza delivery—you really are a man for all seasons," Eden teased him, leading the way to the kitchen.

"Actually, it all falls under the same job description around here."

He set the pizza box in the center of the table and took off his wool jacket to hang on the back of the chair. Eden asked what he wanted to drink and then brought two sodas from the fridge.

Sitting across from each other, they chose their own slices of the gooey, cheesy pizza, and after one bite, Cam said, "Okay, show me your stuff."

"Here? Now?" she asked as if he were suggesting something lewd, venturing a joke for the first time since her faux pas that morning.

She wasn't sure how he would respond but he arched an eyebrow and played along, saying, "I'll take it wherever and whenever I can get it."

"Never admit that," she advised with a laugh, relieved that the pall she'd caused had been lifted.

She handed him the printouts.

Cam took them, finished his first slice of pizza, served himself a second, and then slowly, methodically, set out each sheet of paper on the clear section of tabletop beside him.

As he did, Eden said, "I did three different weights—thin, in case she took control of the weight gain before it got out of hand and went back down—fluffy and more fluffy."

"Fluffy?" Cam repeated with a laugh of his own.

"Okay, chubby and chubbier," Eden amended. "I did the hair light, sort of a cross between blond and gray for the sake of aging, and made the style short—that kind of bubble that older women wear. And I added more of a made-up look on one set and left another set barefaced to cover whether she broke the no-makeup restriction my grandfather imposed on her or stuck with the naked face."

Cam was silently looking closely at each printout.

"What do you think?" Eden asked after a moment. "Look like anyone you know or have ever seen before?"

He didn't answer immediately even then. He took his time with each picture before he said, "There's something familiar about her but I don't know if it's because I've actually seen her before or because there's so much Perry in her."

"Try squinting your eyes a little so it's as if you're seeing her from a distance. Or look more at the overall than at any of the details. Remember the image may only be a *resemblance* to a real person."

Cam squinted his eyes, rearing back in his seat. But in the end he shook his head.

"I still can't place her. What about you? Does she look familiar to you? Or like someone who might have approached you when you were a kid? Or come up to your dad at some point?"

Eden had not only spent many hours with these images, she'd done her own squinting at them and studying of them, so she barely glanced in their direction as she ate the crust of her single slice of pizza.

"I'm where you are—she looks familiar but I'm not sure if that's because I've seen her before or because of the family similarities or just because I've done all this work. By the time I finish one of these projects I know the face so thoroughly that they all end up seeming like someone I know."

"So you're not going to be any help for identifying purposes," Cam said as he finished his second slice and took a third.

"Sorry."

"Maybe we'll have better luck with the rest of your family."

"Maybe. Or with someone else around town. We'll hope so."

Cam bit off the tip of his pizza, washed it down with some soda and then said, "How does your family feel about this, anyway? In the inner circle? The Reverend was pretty uncooperative and made it clear he didn't see any reason to get into all of this, but I haven't had the chance to talk to anyone else."

Eden shrugged, picked off a glob of cheese that had stuck to the inside of the pizza box and ate it with her fingers. Then, in a complete deadpan, she said, "We're all just hoping you never figure out that we've had our grandmother hidden in the basement for the last forty-plus years."

Cam grinned at her and again went along with the jest. "Do you keep her tied up or is she free to walk around and bake cookies?"

"Cookies, for sure. What else are grandmothers for?"

She loved his smile. It was such a great smile. And it was so nice to see it again.

"Seriously," he said then, to get an answer to his question about what her family thought.

"Feelings are mixed," she said. "Probably like your family's feelings were over Karis. You said you were skeptical of her, but were all six of your siblings just as skeptical or were some of them willing to give her the benefit of the doubt?"

"I'd say we all had varying degrees of distrust. I was the worst. Neily and Mara were the most inclined to give Karis a break and not hold her responsible for the money her sister conned us out of. My brothers were all somewhere in between."

"Well, when it comes to my father and my Uncle Carl, they're pretty torn. What they remember of their mother is that she was good to them, that she was the fun parent, the one who would play with them, let them eat candy, not enforce the rules too strongly—"

"All of which probably made living with the Reverend easier," Cam guessed.

"That's the impression I have. They missed her terribly after she left and my dad says he held out hope for a long time that his mother would come back, if only to take him and Carl away with her. But when she didn't, his feelings for her got a little harder. I think on some level my dad and my uncle would like to see Celeste again, but on another level, I'm not sure. It seems like they're kind of worried about opening old wounds."

"And you and your sisters and your cousins?"

They'd both finished eating and Eden went for an éclair she'd brought home from the bakery the afternoon before. She cut it in sections so they could share it for dessert.

"Of the seven of us," she said when they'd each chosen a piece, "there are differing opinions, I guess you could say. Not that any of us are fighting or anything. But my sister Eve and I are kind of middle-of-the-road. We hope Celeste didn't do anything criminal and we're trying to keep an open mind until we know for sure what happened."

"What about your sister Faith?"

"She's completely sympathetic to Celeste. Faith is convinced she understands why Celeste left. Faith felt so restricted herself as the granddaughter of the Reverend that she's sure it was what Celeste felt, too, and that that's why Celeste would do anything—with anyone— to get away."

"And your cousins?" Cam prompted.

"Of Jared, Noah, Kate and Meg? My cousins run the gamut, too—there's some sympathy, some empathy. There's some wait-and-see. And there's some embarrassment and wishing that this whole thing would just go away. But we're all curious, that's for sure. Well, maybe not the Reverend, but he wouldn't admit to having a human emotion to save his own life."

"Not too fond of dear old granddad, huh?" Cam asked.

"You know how he is. The list of clichés is long—fire and brimstone, everything is black-and-white, right and wrong, men are the rulers of the earth, women should know their place, kids should be seen and not heard—it makes him kind of hard to take. He was definitely never a roly-poly grandpa who would pick you up and walk you around the garden."

"So you pretty much think he was the kind of person anyone would want to get away from," Cam surmised.

"I can't imagine being married to him, that's for sure. But then I can't imagine deserting my kids, either, especially when it meant leaving them to that kind of father."

"Yeah, at least when my father deserted my mother and his seven kids he left us to someone kind and loving and nurturing."

"I'm sorry, maybe I shouldn't have said that. About deserting kids. I forgot for a minute that your father ran out on your family."

"Nah, no big deal. I was just making the comparison. It's not a sore spot with me after all this time."

Cam flinched then and raised his elbows to shoulder height, pulling them back and apparently stretching out of a spasm of some kind.

But from Eden's vantage point all she noticed was his impressive chest flexing in her direction, making her itch to reach out and press her hands against it.

So she got very busy clearing away the dinner debris. "Do you want to take the rest of the pizza home?" she asked.

"No, you keep it. I'm not big on leftover pizza," he said as he lowered his arms and rolled his massive shoulders, making her eyes nearly pop out of their sockets to see it.

Then he stood, took his coat from the back of his chair and put it on. "It's after one, I'd better let you get some sleep."

Eden didn't argue that as she closed the pizza box and put it in the refrigerator.

Cam picked up the sheets of paper filled with her day's work, tapped the edge on the table to square them and then held them up. "Thanks for this," he said as he headed for the front door.

Eden followed, her gaze glued to the rear view of shoulders that were a mile wide and looked as if they had the power to easily carry sacks of cement.

"How long before you have the pictures printed up and taped to every storefront window?" she asked as they reached her entryway.

Cam turned to face her and answer her question. "Sometime tomorrow. While they're being copied I'll take one over to the Reverend to show him."

"That's where I'm going tomorrow," Eden said much too brightly as it struck her that they might run into each other.

She knew that shouldn't have thrilled her. That she should have been glad that their time working together was finished, that now they could simply be vaguely congenial neighbors and nothing more.

But she *wasn't* glad their time together was finished and the thought of formal, distant congeniality somehow depressed her.

And that was when she heard herself say, "We could go over to the Reverend's house together…."

Why had she said that?

She shouldn't have.

What was he going to think?

It didn't matter what he thought, she just shouldn't have done it.

He's a cop! she mentally berated herself. *No more cops!*

Then, trying at least to salvage whatever dignity she might have sacrificed with the suggestion, she said, "I mean, he isn't my favorite person in the world, but he *is* my grandfather and he isn't young and it might be hard for him to see the picture of what Celeste may look like. I just thought maybe I—or someone from the family—should be there."

Was she making it worse? It felt as if she was.

But Cam was merely watching her. "Going together might be a good idea," he agreed. "The Reverend won't be happy to see me and maybe being with you will grease my way through the door."

"So you want to, then?" Eden said, trying to sound as if it were inconsequential to her whether he did or not.

"Sure."

"I'm supposed to see him at four tomorrow afternoon. I haven't gotten over there yet but I don't dare drop in so I called and that's the time he said would be convenient for him."

"That'll be the end of my shift so it works for me, too. Why don't I swing by here and pick you up?"

"Okay."

Eden couldn't shake feeling confused and uneasy over what she'd just done and the fact that she shouldn't have and why she had and what Cam's impression of it might be. But if he was aware of her feelings he didn't show it. Instead he just stood there looking down at her, his expression indecipherable.

Then for the second time he raised the papers he held in his left hand. "We worked well together today, I thought," he mused.

"We did," she agreed.

"I enjoyed it."

"Me, too."

"You're sure you don't want to form a partnership and stay in the business?" he asked with a smile that was like warm honey.

Forming a partnership with him had some appeal but not in order to do forensic artwork....

Eden tamped down that notion and shook her head. "Nope, that's it for me. I'm now officially a children's book illustrator and nothing more."

The corners of his mouth quirked up slightly higher and in a voice that was quiet and sexy, he said, "Oh, I don't know, I think you're a whole lot more."

It was on the tip of her tongue to ask what he meant. But she was gazing up into his midnight-blue eyes and for some reason she just couldn't form a sentence. All she could do was stand there as her mind wandered for the third time to kissing him.

He won't do it. He hasn't done it before....

But then his free hand came to the side of her face, cupping her cheek, stroking it with his thumb as he urged her to tilt her head back, as he bent down to press his mouth to hers.

Cam Pratt was kissing her!

And she was kissing him back.

And it didn't matter that his face was stubbly after their long day's work, it only mattered that his lips were parted and sweet, his breath was soft against her skin, his hand was firm but gentle on her face, and oh, could the man kiss! It was no wonder he'd been so popular....

Then it was over and she had to force herself not to strain for another one, to accept that that single kiss was going to be it.

For now...

No, not for now, forever!

Or only for now...

"I'll be here a few minutes before four," he was saying in the midst of her own silent argument with herself.

Eden nodded. "Punctuality is a must," she managed, hoping it made sense when all she could really think about was that kiss she could still feel on her lips.

"I won't be late," he assured.

He opened her door and went outside, and the frigid January air shocked her out of her reverie.

"'Night," he called to her.

"'Night," she echoed, watching him until he'd descended her porch steps and turned toward his house.

Then she closed her door, dropped her forehead to the solid oak panel and groaned.

"What are you doing?" she asked herself.

The answer was that she was doing something she knew—without a doubt—that she shouldn't.

But it was also something she almost felt compelled to do in a way she couldn't begin to fathom.

And because of that, she just wasn't sure she could keep herself from doing it.

"You have to be strong!"

But at that moment she felt stupendously weak.

Weak in the knees after that kiss she wished was still going on....

Chapter Six

Eden knew approximately what time it was when she woke up Thursday morning with a gasp. There was no need to look at the clock on her nightstand or glance at the window to see if the sun was anywhere near rising. She didn't have a doubt that it was between 3:00 and 3:30 a.m.

The same time it had been that first horrible night over a year ago. The same time it had been every night for a while after that. The same time it had been on every other occasion since. Although thankfully those occasions had become so rare that it hadn't happened at all in a few months.

And yet there she was at that moment, wide-awake, her heart beating so hard it was drumming in her ears, her whole head damp with cold sweat, and the awful rush of adrenaline making her want to climb out of her skin.

"I really hate this," she said into the darkness because the sound of her own voice made her feel less alone.

Then she glanced at the clock just for the heck of it. Three-seventeen.

It was a phenomena. No dreams, no nightmares ever preceded it to shock her out of a peaceful slumber. It just happened. Boom! One minute she was sound asleep, the next she was like this. And always between three and three-thirty.

The first time it had happened on that horrible night she guessed it was because she'd had such a close link to Alika. And each time since, she supposed that it was in memory of him.

Tears didn't come with the memories anymore, though. And the grief that had been so bad she hadn't thought she would survive it wasn't as all-consuming. Instead, in the past few months when it happened, it was just something she'd learned to get through.

But why tonight? Why, when she'd gone to sleep thinking about one man, had she been jarred awake on account of another?

Unless going to sleep thinking about the one man *was* the reason.

Thoughts of Cam had absorbed her and made it difficult to fall asleep at all. She'd lain there reliving small things that had happened throughout the day and evening, picturing him, recalling that good-night kiss at her door that she'd chastised herself for and yet fantasized about over and over, longing to have it happen again.

Maybe after that, the wake-up phenomena was her subconscious's way of alerting her to the dangers in her attraction to him. To a man she knew better than to get anywhere near because she knew his type. Too well.

She'd seen it in him in high school and she hadn't spotted anything in him yet to persuade her that he'd changed as he'd matured. Confident, fearless, brash, cocksure of himself and his abilities, his strengths. So cocksure of himself that he'd thought he could skate through physics without putting any effort into it.

It was the kind of personality she'd encountered in more than one cop. In Alika.

And Cam's body that had been buff even in school, that was more buff now? All those amazing muscles he worked for and honed to perfection in the gym above his garage? That was like Alika, too.

Yes, they were wonderful to look at. And yes, when she wasn't guarding against it, her hands itched to be pressed against Cam's powerful pectorals or bulging biceps or those jaw-droppingly impressive shoulders.

But put the physique together with that confidence, that brashness, that take-on-the-world self-assurance, and what was the end product? A magnificently muscled man of steel who might not technically think of himself as a super man, but who, in Eden's experience, did seem to think that if he kept himself in top form he came nearer to being invincible. Indestructible.

When he wasn't.

And she didn't want anything to do with where that could lead.

Or where it could leave her.

Again.

But clearly she had a weakness for that type of man the way someone else might always go for blond guys or guys with hairy chests. Only she wasn't going to give in to that weakness this time around.

She couldn't let herself….

Her pulse was slowing and she was beginning to relax so she stayed in bed, hoping that this would be one of the nights when she'd be able to fall back to sleep.

It just didn't help that she started thinking about that kiss again. About Cam and how good he'd smelled. About the sound of his voice. About how that amazingly handsome face of his got even better-looking when he smiled. About how his dark blue eyes crinkled at the corners, and how white and perfect his teeth were. About the way he ran those big, adept hands through his hair sometimes without even seeming to realize he was….

"But still, no cops," she whispered to herself, repeating what she'd reminded herself of after inviting Cam to go with her to her grandfather's house.

No cops and no police work. She wanted to be as far as she could possibly get from everything to do with them both.

Maybe she'd lost sight of that a little since coming back to Northbridge and becoming reacquainted with Cam.

Cam, who had lived up to his reputation…

The best lips in Northbridge….

One day toward the end of her senior year she'd overheard a group of girls in the restroom talking about him, advising those who hadn't hooked up with him yet to do it before graduation, if only for an evening. No one, the girls-in-the-know had said, should go away to college without kissing "the best lips in Northbridge."

It was a silly schoolgirl thing.

And yet thinking about kissing him in the last few

days, Eden hadn't been able to keep from wondering if there was anything to it.

Now she knew.

There was. There was a whole lot to it.

Maybe not specifically to his lips, but holy cow, did the man know how to use them!

Only finding that out was one thing, she lectured herself as she lay there in her bed. Exploring it any further was something else entirely. Something that she knew better than to do.

Because now it wasn't only a matter of hooking up with the high school heartthrob to test his skills for experimentation and comparison purposes. Now much more was at stake and kissing skills had to be low on the list of priorities.

No matter how good they were.

Oh, who was she kidding? His were great.

It just wasn't enough.

So she decided that this particular three o'clock wake-up was definitely a warning and that she was going to take it seriously.

It was bad enough to have tragedy touch her life once. Nothing could make her court it again. Not even great kisses from a beautifully brawny man. Nothing.

Which meant that once their joint visit to her grandfather was over, it would be the end of her association with Cam. From then on, she would keep her distance. She would be remotely friendly and nothing more.

"And I mean it," she told the ceiling.

She just couldn't go through what she had before.

The best lips in Northbridge or not.

* * *

"Thanks for this. I hope I didn't cut into something important."

"Just unpacking—nothing important," Eden assured Cam as he headed out of town rather than going directly to her grandfather's house Thursday afternoon.

Cam had called her and asked if he could pick her up half an hour early because he had two stops to make before they could see the Reverend at four.

"What do you need to do?" Eden asked.

"Serious police work," he answered. "First I need to make a stop at the Baxter house on a domestic matter."

"Domestic violence in Northbridge?"

"It happens. But this particular problem is domestic without the violence," he said as he parked in front of a small farmhouse close to the main road not far outside of town.

He was driving his own SUV. He hadn't taken one of the police-issue vehicles because, he'd explained, by the time they finished with these two stops and talking to her grandfather he would be off duty. This way he wouldn't have to return to the station. And again the clean, soapy scent of him that infused the car was going to Eden's head.

"Do you want me to wait here?" she inquired when he turned off the engine, not unwilling to bask in the smell that was all him.

"Actually I was thinking that I may need your assistance," he said authoritatively.

That note in his voice raised her curiosity. But knowing that no cop would purposely endanger a civilian, she wasn't worried and simply got out of the SUV when he did.

The farmhouse's front door was unlocked and Cam omitted knocking and simply walked inside. He also didn't announce them once he had, obviously aware that no one was home. The place did have a marvelous smell of its own, though. Sweet and spicy.

"Kitchen," Cam said, pointing a long index finger toward the rear of the place.

"There isn't going to be a body on the floor, is there?"

"Skulls don't bother you but the idea of a body on a kitchen floor does?" he challenged.

"I just want to know what I'm in for."

"No body on the kitchen floor," he said. Then he added, "At least that I know of."

She didn't quite buy the ominous tone in his voice or the frown he seemed to be putting on but she only said, "You first."

"Not so tough now, are you?" he goaded, leading the way.

The house's sweet, spicy smell was stronger in the kitchen. In fact it filled the air. But beyond that and the usual appliances, table and chairs and littered countertops, nothing seemed unusual. Or worthy of a visit from a police officer.

Cam gave no explanations as he opened a few drawers until he found what he was looking for—hot pads. He took them to the oven and pulled that door down, flooding the space with even more of the delicious scent.

"Come and tell me if this is golden enough. I don't bake pies."

"You're kidding?" Eden said.

"Nope, I've never baked a pie in my life," he responded as if she'd been marveling at the fact that he didn't make pastries in his spare time.

"I mean, you're kidding about coming out here to take a pie out of the oven," she clarified despite being fairly certain that he knew exactly what she'd meant.

"Not kidding. Golden or not golden?"

Eden took a closer look. "Golden."

Out came the pie to set on the stovetop and Cam closed the door and turned off the oven.

"Did Marge Baxter honestly call you to come here for that?" Eden demanded.

"She was babysitting her granddaughter, her granddaughter fell and hit her head. Marge had to take her into town for stitches and forgot she'd put the pie in. When she remembered, she called the station and asked if whoever was on duty could come out and do it."

"Serious police work, huh?" Eden said, taking a turn at goading him.

"It would have been serious if the pie had stayed in too long, caught fire and burned the whole house down, wouldn't it?"

Eden just laughed and shook her head. "What's next? Milk left out on the counter somewhere?"

"Teeth," he said, ushering her from the farmhouse.

Since he didn't elaborate, once they were back in his SUV, she said, "If you're going to brush someone's teeth, count me out."

Cam merely smiled a secretive smile.

"Is this all in a day's work around here?" she asked then.

"Some days," he confirmed. Then, instead of telling

her more about their second stop as he headed back to town, he switched subjects and said, "I faxed the age progressions to the police in Bozeman. They'll show them to the waitress who thinks she might have worked with Celeste years ago. She'll tell us if they resemble the woman she thinks might have been your grandmother. If they do but she sees something that should be changed, can you do that?"

"Sure."

That was all the time they had for conversation before Cam pulled to a stop in front of a tiny, boxlike brick house on the very edge of town.

"Reuben Maxwell's house," Eden said. "He can't still be alive and living here?"

"He can and is. At ninety-one. His son Burt lives with him now."

Eden went from looking at the house to looking at Cam. "And we're here on a tooth errand? Let me guess, someone has stolen Reuben's teeth."

Cam shook his head, his dark blue eyes alight with more mischief despite the fact that he was trying to appear very solemn. "It's a case of missing teeth, all right. But Reuben has misplaced them."

"And called the *police?*" Eden reiterated her earlier question.

"Here's how it is." He pretended to be filling her in the way he might a partner. "Burt had to go to Billings on business today. He set Reuben up with everything he needed to be on his own while he was away and called the station, asking if we would look in on the old man. I did that earlier—at noon-hundred-hours—"

"Noon-hundred-hours?" Eden repeated with another laugh, now at his purposely mangling military time.

"That would be lunchtime for you civilians," he said, maintaining his sober countenance as if this was all vitally important. "At noon-hundred-hours everything was going well. But Reuben called an hour ago and reported that he had taken out his teeth and set them somewhere. He can't recall where. Every day at four o'clock sharp, he eats a stick of jerky. He says it's what keeps him ticking and missing a day would be the end of him. But he can't eat the jerky—"

"Without his teeth. So he wants you to find them for him," Eden concluded.

"Life or death. That's what I do, ma'am," he dead-panned.

Eden rolled her eyes but laughed yet again, too. "By all means," she said, waving him on. "Go find Reuben's teeth. But I think I *will* pass on this one."

"If it's more than you can handle, I understand," he said in the same theatrical tone. "I'll leave the engine running so you can have heat."

He got out of the SUV then and Eden's gaze went with him up the walk to the house, appreciating the sight of his broad back encased in his navy wool jacket and the sublime jean-clad derriere below it.

But she was appreciating something else, too. Cam Pratt could be funny. There had only been hints of a sense of humor here and there before but today he was showing her a practically comical side. A side of him that upped his appeal even more because she liked a man who could joke around.

"But no cops!" she repeated what she'd told herself

the day before, again during the wake-up phenomena of the middle of the night, and at least a dozen times while she'd worked today.

The trouble was, at that moment her vow lacked some strength. Seeing him once more, being with him, having him inject some fun and lightheartedness into the mundane aspects of his job, sort of threw a tarp over her resolve. It was still there, but it was camouflaged.

And when she tried to fling back the mental tarp and reexpose the reasons she knew she needed to resist his appeal?

The thought of noon-hundred-hours popped into her head to make her smile.

And that stubborn tarp just wouldn't budge.

"I was under the impression that my appointment today was with you alone, Eden," the Reverend chastised politely as he led Eden and Cam into his living room at four o'clock.

Before Eden could respond, Cam said, "We did the age progression on Celeste's photograph yesterday and I wanted to show it to you. Eden thought you might appreciate having the moral support of a member of your own family when you first saw it."

"I can't imagine why I would need moral support for that. I might have more appreciated the visit I was expecting with only the granddaughter I've rarely seen since she left Northbridge."

Implacable as always, Eden thought.

"Now that I've moved back to town I'm sure we'll be seeing more of each other in the future," she said, although seeing a whole lot of her grandfather was not her goal when his curt, standoffish, overly formal, judg-mental attitude reminded her of how not-particularly-fond of him she was.

"Make yourselves comfortable," the seventy-eight-year-old man invited, motioning to the sofa before he lowered himself into a wingback chair and threaded his fingers together over his flat stomach.

There wasn't an ounce of fat on the elderly man who might have looked unwell were it not for the thick shock of white hair on his head and the alertness of his rheumy blue eyes that let Eden know he still had all his faculties.

He didn't ask them to remove their coats, or show them any other hospitality, however. And he also didn't contribute more conversation to put them at ease. Instead he waited imperiously.

"How have you been?" Eden asked, feeling as if it were her granddaughterly duty to ask.

"Well enough," the elderly man answered.

"Eve said you needed to see your headache doctor in Billings at the start of the week. Are you bothered with those again?"

"Everyone gets a headache occasionally."

So much for small talk. Eden thought Cam was waiting for her to do the family thing before he broached the subject of Celeste again but since the Reverend was being even more peevish than usual, she decided to cut to the chase.

"Maybe you can look at the age progressions now and we won't have to take up too much more of your time."

Cam took his cue, removing the pictures from a manila envelope. But her grandfather didn't spare Cam a glance. His gaze was pointedly on Eden alone.

"I don't know why you agreed to do those things," the Reverend said, referring to the age progressions. "She *is* your grandmother, you know."

After Eve's warning that the old man was unhappy that she was doing the age progression Eden would have been surprised if he hadn't voiced his displeasure with her, so she was braced for it.

"If I didn't do it, someone else would have," she said simply.

"Then you should have *let* someone else do it. Where is your family loyalty?"

"You feel loyalty to Celeste? You never have before," Eden remarked.

"I'm speaking of loyalty to the rest of us."

"I can't see how I'm being *dis*loyal by doing this. We're all curious about her."

"Curiosity killed the cat!" the old man shot out.

Eden wasn't sure what that was supposed to mean or how it was meant to apply. But she didn't see a reason to pursue what seemed like a fit of temper so she said, "Well, I've already done the job and we'd appreciate it if you would take a look at the pictures."

The Reverend glared at her and for a long moment ignored Cam's attempt to hand him the print-outs.

"Please," Eden added but without pleading, merely as a courtesy.

There was another moment of the Reverend staring at her before he faced Cam. But despite the fact that Cam held out the sheets for the elderly man to take, the Reverend didn't accept them, leaving his hands folded over his stomach.

Cam got the message and held up the first age progression of Celeste as if it were a flash card.

One bare glance was all the old man spared before he averted his eyes.

"That's not her," he decreed irascibly.

"Pardon me, Reverend, but there are several possibilities that we need you to look at," Cam said patiently. "Eden tried to cover all the bases and has increased the age by decades to allow for the possibility that Celeste showed up here in the seventies or the eighties or even later. There are also variations in weight. I'd like to show you the rest of the pictures and have you consider if you might have seen someone who resembled any of them over the years. And where and when that might have been."

The Reverend pursed his lips but again allowed his attention to turn in Cam's direction.

Still, each picture Cam showed him was given no time before the Reverend said a curt, "Next." And when they'd gone through them all he merely said a perfunctory, "No." Then he added, somewhat under his breath, "This is a fool's quest."

"Maybe so, but I'm obliged to follow through with it."

Cam tapped the edges of the sheets to the coffee table and then left them there, faceup, in front of the Reverend. "I'm going to leave these here with you. They might spur a memory down the road."

The Reverend steadfastly refused to look anywhere near them.

Eden doubted she could get any further with her grandfather but still she thought she'd make the effort.

"It would be helpful to me if you would take a closer

look at the pictures. You might be able to tell me how they compare with your recollections of the way any of Celeste's family looked. There could be things I could change—"

"I don't remember specifics of the way people looked decades ago," her grandfather said without making any move toward the printouts again. Then, disparagingly, he added, "I thought this was your occupation. I would presume—if you know what you're doing—that you did a competent job of it."

"Part of being competent at it," Eden said, trying to maintain her own patience, "is to gather opinions of people who had contact with the person I'm attempting to portray. Or who had contact with family members who might have had facial similarities. If you think back to the way your mother-in-law looked the last time you saw her and compare that memory with the age progression of Celeste at approximately that age, you might be able to tell me that her mother had begun to be jowly at that point, or that her hair had thinned, or that your mother-in-law was twenty pounds heavier. Then I could add those characteristics."

"I can't tell you anything."

Cam took another stab at it. "Can you at least tell us if the pictures look the way you might have expected Celeste to age?"

"How would I know that?" the Reverend said.

Cam shrugged. "I had an image of the way I thought my wife might look over time based on how her family members had aged."

Cam had been married? Oh.

"I doubt you'll still have that image in your mind

when you haven't laid eyes on the woman or her family in nearly half a century," the Reverend contended, still giving no quarter.

Cam gave the old man an extended cop stare that Eden knew was designed to make him uncomfortable and hopefully inspire him to be more cooperative.

It didn't work. The Reverend was unfazed and finally Cam said, "You've had a while to think since we talked before the holidays. Have you recalled anything? Maybe a Christmas gift Celeste might have sent your sons all those years ago that you'd forgotten about? Or a card you once received that might have been from her?"

"What possible difference would it make even if she did send something when it would have been a lifetime ago?" the Reverend demanded.

"If she did send something and you remembered where it had been mailed from we might have another idea of where Celeste was at one point or another. We could investigate. Every piece—no matter how small—can be important."

"Well, there wasn't anything and I haven't thought of anything else, either. And I'm quite sure I won't. As I told you and Luke Walker when you were here in October, I don't see any purpose in pursuing this. The two men who committed the crimes are both long-deceased, and no one cares anything about Celeste. All you're doing is digging up dirt for no good reason."

"And as we told you, Reverend, this isn't just a local matter. The robbery is a federal issue, the state authorities are involved in Mickey Rider's death, and until every avenue is explored, I'm afraid the dirt is going to be dug up."

The Reverend's glare came to Eden again. "And you're handing them one of the shovels. Shame on you."

Eden wasn't sure what he expected her response to be. Childhood admonishments for fidgeting in church or speaking out of turn would have required a show of contrition. But now she was an adult and in this instance she saw no reason to be ashamed of anything she'd done.

So she angled a glance at Cam and said, "Unless you have more questions, maybe we should go."

"By all means," her grandfather put in before Cam could say anything. "And perhaps next time you ask to visit me it will be just that and not a subterfuge to gain entrance for someone else."

"It wasn't a subterfuge this time," Eden said.

She and Cam stood but Cam bent over and slid the age progression sheets closer to the edge of the coffee table that faced the elderly man.

The Reverend pretended not to notice, his stare unwaveringly straight ahead.

"We'll find our own way out," Eden informed him even though it was obvious the old man wasn't going to escort them.

Neither grandfather nor granddaughter said anything in parting, and Eden and Cam left.

Once they were outside, however, Cam said, "Sorry about that. I didn't expect him to get so PO'd at my coming along."

"It's all right. He's never a barrel of laughs."

"But you probably weren't expecting to get your wrists slapped," Cam insisted as they climbed into his SUV.

"I kind of was. Eve warned me that the Reverend didn't like that I was doing the age progression." She gave Cam a sidelong glance as he drove away from her grandfather's house. "Maybe I should be apologizing to you. But I didn't think the Reverend would make a big deal out of it with someone else there."

"So I was your buffer?" Cam joked.

"No, I didn't *care* that he didn't like what I was doing and I wasn't afraid to get into it with him, I just didn't think he'd bring it up in front of you and I'm sorry if he made you uncomfortable."

"He didn't. I found it all pretty interesting, as a matter of fact."

"In terms of your case?"

"Mmm. What he said to you seemed like it might be more telling than anything he said to me."

"For instance?" Eden prompted.

"For instance," Cam repeated, "that stuff at the start, when he first let you know he was miffed at you doing the age progressions? I was kind of struck by him saying, she *is* your grandmother. He said it as if Celeste was in the other room."

Eden laughed. "You do think we have her stashed in the basement then," she said, referring to what she'd joked about before.

"It just made me wonder if he knows more than he's saying. If he might even know where she is. And there was also that stuff about you giving us one of the shovels to dig up the dirt on Celeste. That would be particularly true if he saw something in one of your pictures that really might lead us to her."

"He hardly looked at them," Eden reminded. "I got the impression that he just thought I should stonewall, like he is."

"Could be," Cam allowed.

"But one way or another, I don't think you got anything you can use, did you?"

"No. But this is the second time I've talked to him and the second time I've left feeling as if he's holding something back."

"He's definitely not being a lot of help," Eden agreed.

"Yeah, he makes it clear that he doesn't want it all brought up again," Cam said. "Not that I blame him."

It was on the tip of Eden's tongue to ask if that was because of something from his own past that he didn't want resurfacing. Like a wife. But she didn't have the courage.

Cam looked at his dashboard clock then and said, "I'm officially off duty now, though, so we don't have to talk about it anymore. We can talk about the Winter Carnival instead."

Not the smoothest change of subject but Eden rolled with it. "I've seen the signs for it," she said.

"It starts tonight. The school is putting it on to raise money for books and computers and to send kids to different events here and there. It'll go through the weekend—there's a spelling bee on Saturday and poetry readings and essay competitions—a lot of educational stuff. But there are a lot of fun things, too, especially tonight. Want to go?"

"With you?" Shock made her blunt.

"Yes, with me."

"I wasn't sure…. I just needed to clarify," she stammered as the sudden invitation began to sink in.

He was asking her to go out with him.

Tonight.

On a date…

She'd sworn she wasn't going to see him again after the visit to her grandfather. But now that the time had arrived she just didn't want to go through with it. Especially not when she had the option not to.

"So what do you say? Want to go?" he repeated.

"I do," she confessed as if it were a dirty little secret, knowing she shouldn't be giving in to what she wanted.

"Do you want to go with *me?*" he asked then, as if her earlier bluntness had made him doubt it.

And while Eden wished she were stronger and wondered fleetingly why she wasn't, she still heard herself say, "Yes, with you."

Cam pulled into the driveway at that moment and turned off the engine before he grinned in her direction. "Give me an hour to shower and change. You can get into the warmest socks and sweaters and coat you have, and we'll go."

Last chance—say no, say you just thought of something else you have to do instead….

But she didn't.

She said, "Okay, sounds good."

Then they got out of the SUV and headed in opposite directions.

And even though, as she crossed her yard, she took herself more to task than her grandfather had ever done, by the time she let herself into her house she was just thinking about which of her socks, sweaters and coats *were* the warmest.

Chapter Seven

Eden thought that Winter Carnival was more like a winter wonderland when she and Cam arrived at the town square that evening. A four-foot snow wall had been erected around the entire park and carved to look like the stone walls of a castle. At the heart of the square, the octagonal gazebo was decorated in hundreds of tiny twinkling white lights and hung inside and out with glittering snowflakes. Tents and booths had been erected—all of them dressed in the lights and snowflakes, as well. And along the path that wove through everything were intricate snow sculptures of children at play, couples strolling, dogs chasing cats, and even an old, hunched-over curmudgeon that reminded Eden of her grandfather.

"This is amazing," she told Cam as they walked the path initially to view each of the sculptures. "I always thought the festivals and celebrations the town did in the square were nice, but I don't remember anything this elaborate."

"It's become a competition," Cam confided. "Everybody wants their event to be bigger and better than the one before. The Ladies' League wants to outdo the Rotary Club. The school wants to do something splashier than the Library Association or the College Alumni. And when the town itself puts on the Fourth of July celebration or the Harvest Festival, the council doesn't want to be shown up by the clubs and organizations, so they go all-out, too. It's becoming an ego thing around here. But we all benefit from the results so no one is complaining."

"Good, because this is spectacular," Eden concluded.

Cam leaned sideways and nudged her with his shoulder. "Maybe next year you can be the artist to do the sculptures and they won't have to bring someone in from out of town."

Eden laughed. "I don't know if snow is my medium, but it might be fun to try."

After their walk through the sculptures they checked out the booths and tents just to get an idea of what there was to buy, test their skills at, and eat and drink.

Booths offered home-baked pies, cakes, cookies, scones, brownies and breads, and one even sold snow cones and flavored icicles. Preserves and canned peaches, pears, pickles and green tomatoes could be had. Quilts, aprons, tapestries, hats, mittens, earmuffs, boalike scarves, and various other craft items made by locals were for sale.

Among the all-winter-related games and activities,

there was fishing through holes in the ice frozen over washtubs, snowman-building competitions, a ring toss with moose antlers as the targets, comically grizzled snow monsters that popped up to have snowballs thrown at them, and a booth where stuffed polar bears could be purchased and then dressed up to suit any whim.

Lamps heated the insides of the tents where bingo and chuck-a-luck games generated money for the school projects, and where a variety of prepared foods could be bought and eaten. Cam and Eden bypassed the hamburgers and fried chicken that were for sale, and instead bought raw hot dogs and marshmallows that they roasted over small outdoor fires tended for that purpose. Hot coffee, tea, cocoa, spiced cider and mulled wine were available just about everywhere they went.

Not only did Eden enjoy the activities and Cam's company, but the carnival also gave her a chance to see more old friends and acquaintances. She was surprised by how many of the people she'd grown up with still lived in the small town or had left for a while and—like her—returned. And certainly it was a boost to her self-esteem to have everyone exclaiming over the improvements in her appearance.

"You're our own hometown Cinderella makeover story," her former history teacher proclaimed, giving Cam something to tease her about from then on.

But by about nine o'clock not even the heat lamps were staving off the chill and when Cam realized she was becoming increasingly uncomfortable, he suggested they go home.

"Feeling the switch from the tropics, huh?" he observed as she sat in the passenger seat of his SUV with her hands clamped between her knees, bouncing her feet in an attempt to warm them.

"I'm *freezing!*" she confessed, giving up on trying to keep her teeth from chattering.

"Maybe I better get you in front of a fire," he said, a touch of concern in his voice.

"Maybe you'd better," she agreed, knowing she'd been tougher than this as a kid but willing to admit to her decreased tolerance of the cold if it meant she was going to get to sit in front of a roaring fire. With Cam.

When they arrived home he suggested they make the fire at her place so she could be inside for the night. Eden agreed to that with zest and ran on feet she was beginning to think might be frostbitten to get in her front door while Cam went to his house for firewood.

He was gone longer than she expected but it gave her time to shed her outdoor gear so she was left wearing only wool slacks and a cable-knit sweater. She made a speedy bathroom stop to fluff her hair and apply a little lip gloss, then she shucked her shoes and changed her socks just because it seemed as if that might help warm her poor feet. She even had a few minutes to tidy the living room a little by stacking packing boxes in a corner. And since she hadn't yet arranged her furniture in any particular order, she pushed her sofa to face the fireplace.

That was when Cam finally rejoined her.

He looked very mountain-manish in his fleece-lined suede coat and gloves, his handsome face ruddy from the cold, carrying split logs under one arm and a thermos under the other.

He dropped the logs into the fireplace and held the thermos aloft. "I thought a couple of hot toddies might help," he said as he set the thermos on the mantel. He removed his gloves and stuffed them into his coat pockets, then he took off his coat.

He was wearing jeans that hugged his hips and a plaid flannel shirt over a thermal T-shirt, only reaffirming the mountain-man image. But it suited him and one look at him almost made her mouth water.

"I'll get mugs," Eden offered a bit belatedly, leaving him to start the fire.

Alone in her kitchen, she took a moment to remind herself that she needed to keep things with Cam purely platonic. No kissing tonight! she told herself firmly. Because while she may have bent her own rule about not having any close contact with him after their visit to the Reverend, this evening was only acceptable if she kept everything platonic. Friendly neighbors. Old schoolmates. Work associates. That was it.

A bent rule was still better than a broken one.

Cam had the fire roaring when she returned. He took the mugs she was carrying and pointed to the couch. "Sit and get warm."

"I'm better, it's just my toes that don't want to thaw," she commented as she took a spot at the very end of the couch and held her still-aching feet out to the heat.

Cam poured two hot toddies from the thermos, gave her one of them and put his on the floor in front of the sofa. Then he surprised her by grasping her ankles in his hands and using them to turn her so that she was sitting with her back to the couch's arm and her feet in his lap as he sat down. Which was when he enveloped her frigid toes in his hands and began a slow, careful massage.

She probably should have complained or pulled away. But how could she when it felt so good to have the heat of his hands infusing her frozen toes? To have the firm, gentle pressure he was applying stimulating her circulation? She was only human and it was taking all the will she could muster not to writhe and moan....

She drew in a breath and quietly exhaled before she said, "That's above and beyond the call of duty, but it's really helping."

"Your toes are so cold I can feel them through your socks. Are you sure we shouldn't have taken you to the emergency room or something?"

And miss out on this? She'd rather risk amputation at a later date than have him stop what he was doing.

"It would take a crane to get me off this couch now," she joked as she wriggled more comfortably into the cushion and sipped her brandy-laced toddy with both hands curled around the mug. "Besides, that would be a rotten ending to a nice night."

He glanced at her from the corner of his eye as he went on rubbing her feet. "You liked the carnival?"

"It's one of the things I came back to Northbridge for."

His brow beetled. "The Winter Carnival?"

"Not specifically, no. But things like it. The whole small town thing—everyone knowing everyone else, events like the carnival, coming home like this afterward to sit in front of a fire—the hominess, the peacefulness of it all, that's what I need now."

"That's why you came back to Northbridge?"

She nodded in the midst of another sip of toddy.

He paused her massage, bent over to pick up his own mug for a drink and Eden chastised herself for the insanity of finding it such a turn-on to have her feet pressed between his chest and his thighs.

Then he replaced the mug on the floor and sat up to continue the massage, obviously unaware of what had just radiated through her.

"Has your life lacked hominess and peace since you left Northbridge?" he asked.

"Small town hominess—yes. That's a special brand that I certainly didn't have in the heart of Honolulu any more than you could have had it in the heart of Detroit."

"True," he agreed.

"And peace? No, I wouldn't say there was that, either. Between traveling around to do forensic work that put me right in the middle of some very ugly, violent crimes and being married to a cop—"

"You were married to a cop?" he repeated, showing his own surprise.

"You didn't know that?"

"No offense, but you haven't been my favorite topic of conversation. Since I've been back in town, if your name came up, I left the room."

"But probably not before saying something like: *I couldn't care less about that bi—*"

"Yeah, something like that," he confirmed with an ornery smile.

"Well, for that, you owe me this foot rub," she decreed, feeling the combined effects of the fire, the toddy and the massage all working to turn her to mush. Which was likely why she was being so talkative about something she might have avoided telling him otherwise.

"So you were married to a cop," he said, clearly trying to encourage her to continue.

"Alika," she said very softly, finding it difficult even now to say it. "His friends called him Al and his last name was longer than you'd be able to say or remember."

She wondered if she would ever be able to think about her late husband without a knot forming in the pit of her stomach.

"And you're a widow—I know that much," Cam said, treading cautiously.

"He was killed in the line of duty, if that's what you're wondering."

"How?" Cam asked, his voice low, quiet, respectful. "Unless you'd rather not get into it."

"It's okay," she said, not quite sure why she felt inclined to candor except that her connection with Alika somehow felt like something she wanted to get out into the air with Cam.

"Along with being a street cop, Alika was on the SWAT team and proud of being the first one in the door on any bust, any raid, any dispute. He bragged about it. But he was the first man in the door one time too many— that particular door was rigged with an explosive device. He busted through it and…" She shrugged and blinked back the moisture that the memory automatically brought to her eyes. "He didn't live to talk about it."

"I'm sorry," Cam said, squeezing her feet in a firm, comforting grip.

He didn't say anything else. He just allowed her the silent support of his touch, letting her decide if they should go on or change the subject.

But now that she'd gotten through the worst of the story, she didn't see a reason not to go on.

So when she knew she could speak again without

crying, she said, "It was a little over a year ago—just before Christmas, to make it even more awful. And between that and my own career, I just came to a point where I decided I'd had enough."

"It isn't only working with skulls and the criminal element that you want to put behind you, then," he said, referring to what she'd told him before. "I'll bet you want cops and everything to do with them behind you, too."

He was a cop and right at that moment she liked having him in front of her, where she could see his handsome profile and where he could go on with that foot massage that had sufficiently warmed her toes but still felt so terrific she didn't want it to end.

But for more than this moment? Yes, she reminded herself, she wanted cops and everything to do with cops behind her, too. And she thought it was only fair to be honest.

"When I met Alika and fell for him and he asked me to marry him, I thought I was the best candidate for a cop's wife. I had close contact with the police and I didn't have any illusions about what went with the job. I didn't go in the way some women do, starstruck by the uniform, not paying any attention to the realities that accompany it, and then unequipped to handle it when it hits them in the face—"

"Hard for those marriages to survive," he said quietly.

"And mine wasn't going to be one of those. I wasn't in for any surprises. Or so I thought."

"But you were wrong."

"The surprise I got was not about the job, it was about Alika himself. And knowing as much as I did actually made it worse."

"You knew too much," he guessed.

"Exactly. I knew how dangerous the situations he was in could be. I knew the extremes of the personalities he could be dealing with. I'd seen some of the worst that could happen to people and I knew it was his job to find whoever had actually done it. I knew that no matter how volatile or violent or depraved they might be, he would have contact with them. I knew that the tables could turn at any time and he might be the next victim whose remains ended up buried in the woods."

Cam grimaced. "I can't imagine that it could have been easy for you to picture him the way you'd seen other—"

"It was horrible. And because I was 'in the business,' so to speak, Alika didn't shield me from anything. He told me what he was doing, when he was doing it—every raid, every bust and when and where it was going down—so I'd spend that whole time watching the clock, my stomach in a knot, terrified that any siren I heard was an ambulance going to the scene to find him hurt, jumping a mile if my doorbell rang because I'd feel as if it couldn't be anything *but* someone there to tell me..."

Her voice caught in her throat and for a little while she couldn't go on.

But after a moment she took a deep breath and continued. "And then one really, really bad night my doorbell rang and it *was* someone telling me the sirens had been for Alika. That they'd come from an ambulance racing to the scene. But that it hadn't mattered...."

Cam let there be silence again while she struggled with her emotions. Then he said, "Did you know your husband was a first-guy-through-the-door kind of cop when you married him? Or was that the surprise you said you got?"

He was very astute.

"That was the surprise," she confirmed. "The private side of Alika was different from Alika-the-cop. He was this charming, laid-back, sweet guy. I knew he worked out and kept himself in great physical condition—that had its own obvious appeal and I thought it was a good thing for a cop to stay in shape. I knew he didn't back down from anything, but the fact that he could handle himself made that seem okay, too. It wasn't until after we were married when I learned that on the job he was very intense. Very hard-nosed and not at all the nice guy I knew. Keeping in shape wasn't just a matter of being in the best physical condition he could be in, it gave him the illusion he was invincible and paved the way for him to be an in-your-face kind of cop."

"A risk-taker *and* an in-your-face kind of cop? Volatile combination."

"And knowing what the job involved, knowing when and where he was in the thick of it, was bad enough, but then to learn about that other side of him, the side that showed no caution, that actually reveled in being the guy who put himself in the most jeopardy—"

"It didn't make for a peaceful life you could just sit back and enjoy. Especially if and when kids entered the picture," Cam finished as if it were something personal to him.

But then he was a cop himself. Here and in Detroit before that. A married cop.

Something about both of those things caused her to sit up, to put her empty mug on the floor, pull her feet so that her heels touched the backs of her thighs, and wrap her arms around her shins.

"So now," he concluded, taking his mug from the

floor, "you've come home to Northbridge where you can feel safe and sound, and not have police work anywhere around you—after this last age progression of Celeste."

She nodded. "The insurance death benefit gave me the financial means to change careers and locations— to change my life—and so that's what I'm doing. Putting distance between me and cops and crime and law enforcement."

"Northbridge is a good place for that. You can illustrate kids' books and what? Look for an accountant for husband number two?" he joked, obviously making an attempt to lighten the mood.

"Give me a nine-to-fiver, that's for sure," she said, glad to take his attempt and run with it even though she was still being truthful. "Someone who comes home from work and talks about building bridges or making research breakthroughs or launching rockets."

"Some superbrain, white-collar guy whose gray matter gets the workout more than his muscle matter," Cam summarized. "I've heard that nine-to-five thing does give you a better edge as husband material," he said with a laugh, making her wonder again about his own marriage.

She hadn't thought of how to ask him about it, though, when he drained the last of his hot toddy and stood.

"I should probably get out of here and let you put those cold toes to bed," he said.

Had he taken that last part of the conversation about her wanting someone who used his brain rather than his brawn as another insult to his own intelligence? She certainly hadn't intended it that way. But she was worried that she might have inadvertently insulted him and she wanted to make sure his negative feelings about her hadn't resurfaced. She stood, too, and said, "You've treated to dinner two nights in a row now. Why don't you let me cook for you tomorrow night and I'll give you a taste of Hawaii in my macadamia nut pie for dessert?"

"Ooh!" he groaned. "Can I have a rain check? I play basketball with the local team and we have a game tomorrow night."

"There's a local basketball team now?"

"No one has told you about the Northbridge Bruisers? I'm crushed." He feigned injury by putting one of those big hands over his heart.

But at least he was back to joking again and Eden thought that was a good sign.

"I'm not much of a sports person," she said, "or I'm sure I would have heard all about the Bruisers or read about you in the sports pages."

"We *are* the sports page the day after a game," he said with mock arrogance.

Then he switched gears and toned down the joking. "Really it's just the guys around here—we get together and play each other for the most part. Football, basketball and baseball, depending on the season. I guess it started up a few years before I came back to town just for the sake of exercise. But now it's become a big deal. We draw a crowd of spectators and everything."

"Maybe I should check it out," Eden said, because while she genuinely didn't have any knowledge of or interest in sports of any kind, the idea of watching Cam did have an appeal.

"We usually make a night of it. After the game we all end up at Adz—that's the restaurant-slash-sort-of-

English-pub that Ad Walker turned the old hole-in-the-wall bar into. If you hate the game you could reward yourself with that part afterward and see some more people, wow them with your Cinderella makeover," he teased. "Or if you want to skip the game altogether, you could just go to Adz later on."

Those were suggestions, he wasn't inviting her. And Eden's concern that she'd offended him niggled at her again. Not that he owed her any kind of invitation, or that just because they'd been out tonight they were dating or anything, she reminded herself, trying not to feel disappointed that he *hadn't* asked her to go to the game. With him...

"I'll have to see how tomorrow goes," she said non-committally.

Cam took his mug to the mantel and set it there. His coat was draped over the edge of the hearth and he retrieved it to put it on. Then he took his thermos from the mantel.

"How do the toes feel?" he asked as he headed for the front door with Eden following behind.

"Much better. Warmer and they don't hurt anymore. Anytime you're giving out foot rubs I'll be in line. I think you may have missed your calling."

"Don't let word get out or that'll be the next thing I have to do on the job around here—stop and rub somebody's feet."

Eden laughed at that. "Hey, if you can take pies out of ovens and find dentures, what's a foot massage now and then?"

"I only rub very special feet," he confided as they reached the door and he turned to face her.

Why did the man have to look like that? she asked herself as she took in those ruggedly gorgeous features and those blue-black eyes that actually seemed capable of increasing her body temperature with one glance.

And why did he have to be looking at her the way he was? With more than a simple glance, studying her with a gaze so penetrating it was as if he could see right into her mind where all she could think about was the kiss of the previous night and how good it had been and how much she wanted him to do it again in spite of every argument she could make against it....

"Thanks for tonight," she said then. "I had a great time."

"Yeah, I did, too," he said quietly. "I'm gonna hang on to the rain check for the macadamia nut pie, though. Don't think I'm letting you off the hook."

"Anytime," she said, mimicking what he'd said to her the night he'd helped her with her power outage even as she was telling herself that it was for the best that he hadn't taken her up on that offer for the next night, best that they honestly did go from here to being only friendly neighbors because he *was* a cop and not a nine-to-five....

But there he was, tall and broad-shouldered, a fabulous-looking power to be reckoned with in that suede coat, and when his free hand came up to the side of her face, the last thing she was thinking about was his brain or his job or what he might talk about when he got home from work every day.

She was just thinking that she hoped that big, strong hand was there as a beginning and not as a parting caress....

And then it guided her face toward his as their mouths met exactly as Eden had been dying for them to.

Well, not *exactly,* because she'd been dying for a kiss like the one of the previous evening's end and tonight's was different than that one. Tonight's was even better.

His lips were parted right from the start, freeing hers to part, too. And once they had, his tongue joined the festivities.

Tentatively at first. Testing the waters. Teasingly darting in and then retreating as if it might not come at all.

Except that the next time it did, Eden's tongue was poised and met it, tip to tip, in a way that made the kiss so much sexier.

Her head fell farther back and he took full advantage of it, opening his mouth wider, sending his tongue to play bold and brazen games that inspired hers to keep pace, to do some teasing and a whole lot of tempting of her own.

She raised her hands to his chest—inside his coat—feeling those hard pectorals beneath the flannel of his shirt.

His hand slipped around to the back of her head, supporting her against an even deeper turn of their kiss, of his tongue that was exploring now, decisive and dominating and setting things inside her alive that hadn't been in a very long time.

The best lips in Northbridge? He had more than that going for him, Eden thought as she got lost in the sensations, the arousal he was creating with nothing more than his tongue and the hand that was massaging her head more sensually than it had her feet.

Who cared if he could do physics when he could kiss like that? The man was a master!

And she would have done just about anything to have it go on and on.

Which, of course, it couldn't. Not without going even further. Not without evolving into more than kissing. Not without proving that she didn't have any control at all.

And she needed to have some control, she warned herself. She *needed* to....

So she forced those hands at his chest to push against him, just enough to let him know they needed to put on the brakes.

He got the message and began a retreat that flooded her with regret. First his tongue said a brief farewell to hers. Then his lips were gone and back again in a much more chaste kiss that segued to a complete ending.

His hand eased her head forward so he could kiss only her forehead then, his breath hot in her hair for a brief moment before he took his hand away and stood straight again.

And that was it.

"Good night," he said simply, opening her door and letting himself out into the cold January air.

"Good night," Eden said after him, unsure if he'd even heard her over the sound of her screen door closing behind him.

She ignored the chill that was overtaking her again as she stood there, though, because it wasn't temperatures that were on her mind.

It was the fact that while he had suggested she might want to check out his basketball game, they had no actual plans to see each other again.

What if that earthquake of a kiss was only his way of leaving her with something to remember him by because, when it came to socializing, he had every intention of keeping *his* distance from her from now on?

That would save her from herself, she thought. It would force her to abide by her own rule. To keep her anticop vow.

It would be a good thing.

Except that the idea of Cam staying away from her made her desperate for that not to be the case....

Chapter Eight

It was six-thirty Friday evening when Cam arrived home from work. He had less than half an hour to grab something light to eat, change out of his uniform and get to his basketball game.

Intent on eating first, he went directly to his kitchen, trying to decide whether to microwave some soup or whatever leftovers were in the fridge. But as he got to the back of the house the motion-detector light over Eden's garage turned on and curiosity pushed him to the window above the sink instead.

Eden was approaching her garage, hauling a packing box.

Cam watched as she climbed the steps to the upper deck and propped the box between her hip and the stair railing so she could open the door to the space she'd mentioned she was going to use as an art studio.

That didn't look like something she would be doing if she intended to go to the basketball game tonight, he thought.

Disappointment slammed him like a body blow.

But he knew he didn't have any right to that feeling. Or any reason to care what Eden did or didn't do tonight.

The time had come for them to go their separate ways—that's what he'd decided the evening before and nothing had changed to make it any less true now. She had her own life, her own ideas of how it should play out from here and with what kind of guy, and he had his life. And the only connection that there could be between the two of them was that they were neighbors.

Despite that, though, he continued to spy on her as she went into the studio and turned on the lights.

He could see her through the large window that matched the one in his workout room as she set down the box. Then she came back out again, leaving the lights on as she returned to the house.

She was probably going to bring out more boxes....

And there he waited, knowing he shouldn't, that he didn't have the time to spare, telling himself to get his ass in gear, and yet he remained standing at the sink when she came into sight again with the second box a moment later.

She looked great. As always. Her shiny burnt-umber colored hair was twisted up the back of her head and curls sprang to life at her crown. She had on a short jacket that hid whatever she was wearing under it. But it ended at her waist and allowed him a view of the jeans she had on. And they were something to see. Or at least the way they looked on her was something to see. Snug through the hips, they grazed her rear end so tantalizingly it nearly made him drool.

And why he was standing there torturing himself, he honestly didn't know.

But still he stayed where he was as she made trip number three.

It *was* torture, though. Looking out that window at her just made him want to be with her even worse than he had all day long. Not to mention all night last night after he'd left her place. He wanted to rush outside and offer to help her carry boxes. He wanted to do what he'd kept himself from doing the previous evening and ask her to go to the game with him, to Adz afterward. He just wanted to be with her.

And he couldn't be.

Not if he had any sense at all.

When she'd told him about her late husband, when she'd told him she didn't want anything to do with another cop, he'd known for sure that there could never be anything between them.

Too much of what she'd said about being a cop's wife could have come from Liz's mouth during their marriage. Listening to Eden say it again had left him thinking one thing—*get out of here before it's too late.*

Which was why he'd finished his hot toddy and headed for the door. Why he hadn't asked her to go to tonight's game with him.

Cut your losses, he'd advised himself. And he'd acted on it.

Then he'd stood in her entry, looked down at her, and he'd been sunk.

But okay, so he'd kissed her, he thought as his gaze

stuck with her on her fourth trip to the garage. Kissing her had just been an uncontrollable lapse. Something that he couldn't explain. A draw he hadn't been able to resist even in the middle of telling himself he had to.

But when that kiss had ended?

As amazing as it had been—and damn, it *had* been amazing—he'd forced himself to remember what he knew even now he had to keep in mind at all costs.

He had to remember that there was a gap between them. That there had been a gap between them when they were teenagers, and that the gap was still there. That Eden was physics and he was football—figuratively, anyway. And that while that gap might not be as obvious when the whole attraction thing was in play, in the long run it was still a gap.

A gap made all the wider by the fact that he was in the one occupation she absolutely didn't want in her life—he was a cop. Which was what he would always be. Because he already knew he couldn't be happy as anything else. Regardless of how much might be riding on it.

So when it came to Eden, he had two strikes against him and one strike had been enough to tank a whole marriage.

Which meant that that kiss—that damn amazing kiss—had to be his parting shot.

Like it or not...

Somewhere in the process of watching Eden carry boxes out to her studio, he'd grasped the edge of the sink. But now his fingers were cramping with the force and it sent a message to him to stop what he was doing. To stop looking at what he couldn't have. To stop thinking about what he couldn't change. To stop wanting to be with Eden.

He used his grasp of the sink to finally shove himself away as she headed for her house yet again.

One glance at the clock on the stove let him know he didn't have time to eat now. He didn't care. The appetite he'd had when he'd come in was gone anyway.

But as he headed for his bedroom to change his clothes, he wished his craving for Eden was as easy to shake.

Because it wasn't.

Nothing helped. Not the fact that he had a clear understanding of why he couldn't pursue anything with her. Not the fact that he was determined not to feel the way he did. The craving still went right along with him to the bedroom.

The craving and the hope that she might show up tonight after all.

Even though he knew it could mean disaster if she did.

"Well, well, well."

Eden glanced at her sister Eve as they left the high school gymnasium after the basketball game and got into Eve's car to go to Adz.

"Well, well, well, what?" Eden asked.

"You have a thing for Cam Pratt."

"I do not."

Eve smiled knowingly and started the engine. "Do, too. I was surprised that you called and showed an interest in this game tonight. You hate sports. But I thought, it's Friday night and maybe you just wanted to get out a little—even though I know you already *got out a little* last night at the Winter Carnival because the whole town was buzzing with that information today. Still, I thought it was good that you feel like socializing and reconnecting with people around here. And this is part of what I was looking forward to about you moving back to Northbridge—having a sister to hang-out with. But tonight wasn't any of that. Tonight was you wanting to see Cam Pratt play basketball."

"You're crazy," Eden claimed.

It didn't put her sister off the scent.

"Your eyes were glued to him from the minute we walked in. Even when he was over by the bench, toweling off, and the action was at the other end of the court, you were looking at him."

Especially when he was toweling off. When his short-sleeved T-shirt had been clinging to his shoulders, chest and back. When his bulky arms and thick thighs had been all pumped up. When his face had been glistening with sweat and his hair had been damply waving on his head, and still he'd looked so sexy she'd hardly been able to breathe....

Eden tried to push the memory out of her mind.

"You're imagining things," she accused her sister rather than admit to the truth. It was bad enough to give in to anything that fed this irrational attraction she had for Cam—like going to his basketball game to ogle him. It was worse to confirm her sister's suspicions of it. Somehow that seemed as if it would add substance and make it even harder to get the attraction to calm down and—hopefully—fizzle out eventually. Which was Eden's ultimate goal.

"Even the Reverend said it," Eve persisted.

"Said what?"

"He asked me if there was something going on with the two of you when I took him to the bus station tonight."

"I don't know why the Reverend would think that anything was going on with Cam and me," Eden said.

"He thinks it because you brought Cam with you yesterday and then went to the carnival with him afterward—yes, even the Reverend heard about it."

"I'm surprised that, with all that's going on, Cam and I are what he talked about."

"Oh, believe me, he talked about plenty," Eve said.

That sounded like an opening for a change of subject and Eden took it. "What else did the Reverend say? Anything about the age progression?" she asked.

"The Reverend said he couldn't believe you'd gone through with doing it. That he put the pictures in the trash when you left yesterday because he didn't have any intention of looking at them again—*ever.*"

"So he isn't going to cooperate at all," Eden said.

"You can't really blame him, can you?" Eve asked.

Eden glanced at her sister. "Are you thinking that finding Celeste would be better left alone, too?"

Eve shrugged. "The old man is a bear—there's no question about that. But this has to be hard on him and he's *seventy-eight*—that isn't young. Sure, I'm curious about our missing grandmother and it might even be interesting to meet her. But is it worth it? I mean, if she's still alive she must have a life of her own. The Reverend has what's left of his. Nobody is being harmed now by anything that happened in 1960. Why not let sleeping dogs lie?"

"It isn't up to me. Or even the local cops. The FBI and the state authorities—"

"I know, I know, I've heard it more than once."

"And are you unhappy with me, too? For doing the age progression?" Eden asked, wondering this for the first time because her sister hadn't voiced an opinion before and now there seemed to be a note of annoyance in her tone.

"I wouldn't say I'm unhappy with you, no. Just…" Eve shrugged again. "I'm just not sure it serves a greater good. I'm not mad that you did the age progression or anything," she added amiably enough to let Eden know she meant it. "But it *is* poking the bear with a stick. And yesterday I guess the Reverend saw you as the Trojan Horse—the decoy who brought the enemy into his sanctuary when he was only expecting the granddaughter he hasn't seen in a long time."

"Cam isn't the enemy. He's just doing his job and, believe me, I've seen it done with much less patience."

That had come out too defensively and it made Eve grin as if Eden had just shown her poker hand.

Before her sister could say anything, Eden continued the defense—her own—knowing she was only compounding things and yet unable to stop herself.

"Cam and I worked on the age progression together. He said he had to show it to the Reverend, I said I was going there to visit and he might as well come along. That way the Reverend wouldn't have to see the pictures I generated of Celeste without someone from the family being with him. I don't think that's bringing the enemy into camp. And Cam could have been much more aggressive than he was. He could have pressured the Reverend, made threats and insinuations to scare him into cooperating—I've seen it done, especially with someone being as uncooperative as the Reverend."

They'd reached Adz and Eve parked nose-first in a spot on Main Street not far from the place.

"So you whisked Cam out of harm's way and took him to the carnival?" Eve joked to goad her.

Eden rolled her eyes. "Yes, I *whisked* Cam out of harm's way," she said facetiously. Then she continued her explanation. "The Reverend was acting as if he didn't want to see me any more than he wanted to see Cam or the pictures. So I cut the visit short. As for the carnival, that was a last-minute thing, nothing to set tongues wagging."

Although if anyone had seen Cam sitting on her couch afterward, rubbing her feet, tongues would have had even more to wag about. And if anyone knew about the kiss that had ended the evening? There had been considerable tongue action in that!

Just the brief recollection of that kiss was enough to light a bit of fire in Eden. The same fire that she'd gone to bed with after Cam had left the night before, that had kept her sleepless until three this morning.

But her downplaying diatribe only seemed to amuse her sister. "You definitely have a thing for Cam and that's why you wanted to go to the game tonight."

Apparently talking about their mutual grandfather had only succeeded as a distraction to a point. Now they'd come full circle.

Eden again attempted to downplay what was really going on. "I heard about the game tonight—you're right, it *is* Friday night and I did feel like getting out. The game just seemed like a good way to do it. That's all there is to it."

"It was a way to get out and see Cam at the same time."

"We could have gone to the carnival, that would have been fine with me," Eden lied.

"But you didn't *suggest* the carnival, did you? You suggested the game."

Eden sighed and tried a new tack to convince her sister she wasn't interested in Cam. "He's a cop, Eve. I don't want anything to do with another cop. You know that."

Eve pursed her lips together in a sad, sympathetic smile. "So you like Cam but you're fighting it and gawking at him from a distance, letting yourself see him without being with him."

Sisters. Sometimes they knew too much even without being told.

Still, Eden didn't open up. Instead she said, "There's also something from years ago that's an issue. I wasn't very nice to Cam when I tutored him in physics senior year and he's never forgotten it. Put the two things together and nothing is going to ever make us anything but neighbors."

Neighbors who happened to get swept up in the kiss of the century last night....

But Cam hadn't asked her to go with him to the game tonight and Eden reminded herself of that, of the likelihood that he didn't want anything more to do with her, kiss or no kiss.

"Cam is a good guy, Eden," Eve said then, taking up his defense.

"So was Alika," Eden countered.

"He was," her sister agreed matter-of-factly. "We all loved him. But just because he was a cop and Cam is a cop—"

"Is reason enough for me not to have anything to do with Cam," Eden concluded.

"Not even if you really want to?" Eve said.

"Not even if I really want to."

"Instead you're just going to watch him from the sidelines?"

"Yes," Eden said firmly.

Eve shook her head, obviously skeptical about how successful that was going to be. But all she said was, "He really is a good guy."

"I'm glad for him. But I'm not interested."

"Then maybe we should just grab a pizza and go home," Eve challenged.

Eden's expression must have been enough of a response because before she'd said anything, Eve said, "Yeah, that's what I thought."

Then Eve got out of the car and waited for Eden to join her to go into Adz.

Where Cam either already was or would be soon.

Eden knew that if she got out of the car, too, she would be confirming her sister's suspicions for sure and she told herself to stay in the car, to roll down the window and tell Eve to get back in, that they'd go for pizza....

But in the end she got out of the car.

Eden had been at Adz for forty-five minutes before Cam showed up. Long enough for her to worry that his plans had changed, that he wasn't coming at all.

But then there he was, freshly shaved and showered, his hair combed back on top, wearing jeans and a navy-blue V-neck sweater with a white T-shirt underneath it.

One look at him made her feel as if her blood pressure had increased.

Nothing else happened, though. Beyond her own un-detectable-to-the-naked-eye physical reaction and an elevation of her spirits, she didn't approach him and he didn't approach her. Which made those elevated spirits nose-dive and, after another forty-five minutes of watching him only on the sly, of seeing him take the long way to the bar rather than get anywhere near where she and Eve and even his own sisters were sitting, Eden decided she might as well suggest to Eve that they leave.

But just as she was going to do that, the subject of the new pool table came up.

Adz had, in the last week, expanded into the vacant storefront next door and added a pool table. And Eve offered the information that Eden was uncommonly good at the game.

Near enough to hear that news was Steve Foster— one of the bullies who had made Eden's senior year hellish. Unlike Cam, Steve Foster had talked to her tonight in order to tell her how amazing it was that anyone as ugly as she'd been could look the way she did now. Eden hadn't known whether she was supposed to thank him for the backhanded compliment or not, but had ended the conversation as soon as possible, thinking no more highly of him than she had before. But when he overheard that she could play pool, he was inspired to challenge her to a game.

At least the pool table was in another room, Eden thought, and she wouldn't have to go on witnessing Cam's efforts to stay away from her. And since she also thought it would be satisfying to beat Steve Foster at anything, she accepted the challenge.

Which was how she ended up playing several games

and drawing a whole lot of attention from everyone except Cam.

"I'll play winner," was the call toward the end of each game and since Eden kept winning long after she'd trounced Steve Foster, she kept playing.

And maybe hoping just a little that one of the "I'll play winner" calls might come from Cam.

But when, game after game, it didn't, she finally gave up and announced that, win or lose, the seventh game was going to be her last.

That was when Cam's deep, rich baritone sounded from somewhere behind the group that had gathered to watch. "Oh, come on, just one more."

Eden sank the last shot of the game she was playing at that moment and glanced around the room in search of him. He was leaning against the wall just inside the poolroom door.

"With me," he added when their eyes met, as if that somehow sweetened the deal.

It did, of course, but still he couldn't be privy to that fact, so she said, "I don't know. I think I've had enough."

He pushed off the wall and crossed to the rack that held the cues, choosing what he wanted. "Just one more," he repeated in a tone that brooked no refusal.

Eden wondered why he'd come into the poolroom when he'd gone to such lengths to avoid her in the restaurant earlier. Had he finally decided to seek her out and was using pool as his excuse? Or could he just not resist attempting to beat her?

Not that it mattered because she wasn't going to run, so she said, "Maybe *just one* more."

And made him smile a satisfied smile.

She'd drawn quite a crowd of onlookers by then but when Cam stepped to the opposite end of the table everyone else in the room seemed to fade away, leaving her only aware of him.

Even though she barely looked at him. After ignoring her, he had no more than that coming, she decided, focusing instead on taking the pool balls from the pockets.

As she racked and positioned them, she said, "Do you want to flip a coin to see who breaks?"

"Call it," he said, skipping any other amenities.

She finally took a look at him now that he was closer, fighting the shiver of appreciation that went through her at how staggeringly handsome he was.

"Heads," she said, hating that her voice cracked and gave away the fact that, when it came to him, it took so little to unsettle her.

Cam flipped a quarter, caught it and turned it onto the back of his hand. "Heads it is. Your break."

Eden chalked the tip of her cue and positioned the cue ball.

While she lined up her shot, he said, "So you're a pool shark, huh?"

If he was purposely trying to disturb her concentration he didn't need to bother. His paying attention to her was enough to do that. She just wasn't going to let him in on that morsel of knowledge, either.

"I haven't taken anybody's money," she answered as she leaned over the table's edge and broke for their game. When her three-ball went into the side pocket— and still hunched over her cue—she raised only her eyes to him and added, "Yet."

"Whoo-hoo!" he said with a laugh. "Do you want to put a wager on this?"

Eden straightened up. "I don't know, I'd feel kind of bad taking a cop's hard-earned pay."

"Because you're so sure you'll win," he said, grinning a slow, confident grin. "Maybe we should bet something besides money."

"Like what?"

He shrugged a broad shoulder. "Winner's choice?"

"That could end up being pretty high stakes."

"Worried you'll lose?" he asked.

"No," she answered without hesitation.

"You're not worried because pool is a game of physics and you figure you have me beat going in?" he said with no shortage of cockiness.

"I'm not worried because I'm good," she said with a small smile and some cockiness of her own.

"Well, I'm willing to let the winner name the prize, if you are," he said.

Eden mimicked his shrug. "Okay," she responded.

Then she took her second shot. She hadn't called her first shot but she did the next one and from then on, just to show off. And as she'd done in most of the games tonight, she ran the table, pretending she didn't even notice he was there when the truth was she knew every time he switched his weight from one hip to another, every time he thumbed the tip of his cue, every time he moved out of her way for a shot.

She also knew that he once more smelled of soap and maybe shampoo because when he didn't move too far away she caught whiffs of it. And since each whiff went to her head, she thought that might have been the reason she scratched with only her five ball and the eight ball keeping her from beating him without ever letting him shoot at all.

"Ooh, the master scratches and now we have a game," he goaded as he stepped to the end of the table to take his turn.

· It was no wonder he was so cocky. He was good, too. Every bit as good as Eden was and with each ball that glided into a pocket she came closer to thinking he was going to be the one to ruin her streak of wins.

And then, with only her five ball and the eight ball left on the table, he missed the shot at the eight ball that would have given him the victory.

He flinched as the eight ball stopped at the edge of the corner pocket. "Ohh! Almost!" he wailed.

"But almost isn't enough," Eden said as she stepped up.

He hadn't left her an easy shot. Her five ball was close to the eight and the eight was teetering on the corner pocket. A breeze could have knocked it in and if that happened before she got her five ball in she'd lose.

Eden studied the shot from every angle. None of them gave her much advantage and she finally decided she just had to shoot and hope for the best.

Smooth and light, she advised herself as she chalked the tip, trying not to think about the fact that all eyes— especially Cam's—were on her.

Then she did a bit of a contortion to get to the cue ball and made her shot.

The eight ball stayed where it was but the roll of the five was painfully slow and she held her breath, afraid she hadn't tapped it hard enough, willing it to go all the way.

Come on... Come on...

In! The ball hit the hole and dropped.

She must not have been the only one to hold her breath because the moment the ball fell the silence of the room was filled with some laughs, some cheers, some clapping, and a few Awws from whoever had been pulling for Cam to beat her.

Eden pretended it was all a matter of course for her as she hit the cue ball again, sank the eight and watched the cue ball bank off the rail just beyond it and sail away to give her the win.

Cam seemed to take the loss in stride because there was still a smile on his delicious face when she looked up at him as the onlookers began to disband.

He inclined his head and said, "I had you going there for a while, though, didn't I?"

"Your run was the full seven balls, I scratched after six, so yes, you did have me going. For a while," she conceded.

"And now you're done? We could go two-out-of-three."

She'd won and she knew what she was going to exact as her prize so rather than risk it, she said, "Are you trying to worm your way out of paying up?"

"Guess that'll depend on what the winner's choice is," he answered, sounding undaunted. "But if you don't want to play anymore why don't we turn the table over to the next game and talk about what losing is going to cost me on the drive home?"

"You're driving me home?"

"Eve was ready to leave so I told her I would," he said as they relinquished their cues to the next players.

That didn't tell her whether it had been Eve's idea or his and Eden wondered about it. It was impossible to know. But Eve was, indeed, gone when they returned to the restaurant portion of Adz.

Cam leaned to his side and said, "See, I told you," as if he'd known she'd been looking for her sister. Then he said, "I'm ready to go if you are."

"Sure," Eden agreed.

"Get your coat and I'll get mine and I'll meet you at the door."

They wove separate paths to accomplish that before ending up on the sidewalk that bordered a deserted Main Street.

But once they were out of the noisy restaurant Eden couldn't resist asking. "So whose idea was it that you take me home? Yours or Eve's?"

"Does it matter?"

"I'm betting it was Eve's since you stayed away all night. And if that's the case, maybe I should walk home."

"It wasn't Eve's idea, it was mine."

"How come?"

He shrugged. "I was staying away from you because you said last night that you didn't want anything to do with a cop. I thought I'd give you some space."

"Then you changed your mind?"

A second shrug. "I just couldn't go through with it. I felt too guilty keeping all the cookies for myself."

"Huh?" she said, airing her confusion.

"Marge Baxter sent me a box of homemade chocolate chip cookies as thanks for taking her pie out of the oven yesterday. I knew I should share them with my partner for the job but it was tough. I was tempted to hog them all. In the end, I guess I just couldn't do it."

In other words, what had occurred to her the night

before after their kiss had been true—he *had* intended to keep his distance from her. But he hadn't been able to follow through with it. Any more than she'd been able to follow through with her own vows to stay away from him.

Well, for tonight at least. She really was going to try to do better tomorrow.

But until then?

"Chocolate chip cookies, huh?" she said.

He grinned at her as if he knew she'd seen through him and didn't mind. "Homemade," he repeated. "They're in my car. We can go to your place and divvy them up."

"And I can tell you what I want for winning that pool game," Eden reminded, trying not to analyze why she suddenly felt as if she were on top of the world.

Chapter Nine

"These are the best chocolate chip cookies I've ever eaten," Eden raved as she took her third from the open box on her coffee table.

"Marge has won awards for them," Cam said as he dunked his fourth in milk.

They'd been back at Eden's house for less than half an hour but they'd settled in on her sofa, angled to face each other, cozily munching the treats. Conversation on the drive from Adz had been about where each of them had learned to play pool. Since coming inside their attention had been on how best to enjoy the cookies, so Eden had yet to get into what she wanted from him as her prize for beating him. She was just about to when he said, "I heard from the Bozeman police tonight. There was a message on my cell phone when I came out of the locker room shower and I called back before I got to Adz."

That must have been why it had taken him longer than the rest of the team to join everyone at the restaurant, Eden thought, glad to know that the possibility of seeing her hadn't made him drag his feet.

"Have the Bozeman cops shown the age progression of Celeste to the waitress who thinks she might have known her?"

"They have. I was going to call you about it tomorrow but since I have you here now—"

"I hope the waitress was more cooperative than the Reverend."

"She was. She told them that there's enough of a resemblance for her to believe even more that the woman she worked with all those years ago and knew as Charlotte Pierce really was Celeste. But she says we're not quite on-the-money with the picture. Any chance you could come in tomorrow and make some changes?"

Eden battled instant elation. She'd hated ending the previous evening without any firm plan to see him again today. If she agreed to go into the police station to work on the age progressions again she would know for sure that she'd be with Cam again tomorrow and that excited her far more than it should have. This was getting out of hand, she told herself.

But she only said, "I'm free tomorrow. Where did I go wrong?"

"Hair and weight, but the hair was wrong because of a problem in the first report they sent. I don't have the details yet, but there was some mistake—a typo or something—so the hair isn't right at all. Plus we didn't beef her up enough. We need to add at least fifty— maybe even seventy-five—pounds. Anyway, the Bozeman guy will fax me a copy of what the waitress said after seeing the pictures and we can go over it tomorrow. Hopefully without any errors this time."

"At least *fifty*—and maybe *seventy-five*—more pounds? Celeste really did gain," Eden marveled. "That takes her out of the fluffy-grandma-body and puts her into a whole other weight category."

"It would make her pretty big," Cam agreed.

"And because we share the same genes, I guess I won't have another cookie," Eden said since that was what she'd been considering.

Cam laughed and let his gaze drop briefly to the snug-fitting, bright yellow scoop-neck sweater she was wearing over a lacy camisole. "I don't think you have anything to worry about," he said with enough appreciation to please her.

But still the thought of a grandmother who could be very large made her decide against any more cookies and instead she stood, brought a dish of sugar-free mints from the kitchen and popped one of those instead.

"Is that the best response you've had from the age progressions so far?" she asked when she rejoined Cam on the sofa.

He must have had his fill of cookies and milk, too, because he set the glass on the coffee table and took a mint. "Yeah, it is. We have the pictures posted all over town and we're canvassing the neighborhood, but nobody's come forward with any sightings or information."

"What about you? You thought there was something familiar in the pictures when I first did them. Nothing came of it?"

"No. It's still eating at me but I haven't been able to

pin anything down, either. I'm hoping maybe the changes will get me—or someone else—closer to figuring out if and when and where Celeste might have actually been around."

"Don't count on anything from my grandfather. Eve saw the Reverend late today and he told her he threw the pictures away without looking at them again. Apparently he's really mad at me for doing them at all. And for bringing you there yesterday, too."

"I know we hit a sore spot but it couldn't be helped."

"He's probably praying for your eternal damnation as we speak," Eden joked.

"Yours, too, for doing the progressions," he countered.

Eden laughed. "No doubt."

There didn't seem to be any more to say on the subject and Eden felt that freed the way for what she was more interested in.

"So. We've established that I honed my skills as a pool player in my college dorm because I was still too much of a dork to be asked out on dates, and that you learned in a Detroit bar frequented by your cop buddies. But we haven't established what I won tonight."

"Uh-oh. Time to pay up, huh?" he said.

"This is it," she confirmed.

"Am I going to have to run around the block naked or something?"

Now *that* was an alluring idea that instantly made her imagine what it might be like to see him completely in the buff....

But she shied away from that notion before it whetted too much more of her appetite and said, "Nope, what I want is the lowdown."

His brow beetled. "The lowdown on what?"

"You've said a couple of things about being married and I didn't know you were. I want the story."

His response was an exaggerated grimace. "You don't want to hear that."

"Yes, I do. Come on," she cajoled. "A bet is a bet and I told you about Alika. It's your turn."

He still didn't leap to satisfy her curiosity. He hesitated, stretching an arm along the top of the couch cushions and making another pained expression before he said, "Yes, I was married. To a woman named Liz Stanley. We met on a sort-of-blind date arranged by an army buddy when we were on leave."

"In Detroit?"

"In your backyard, actually—we had a week's leave in Waikiki. It was at the end of our tour of duty and my buddy was engaged, so he and his fiancée decided it would be romantic to get married there. His fiancée, a few family members from both sides and a couple of friends were willing to make the trip. Liz was the maid of honor. I was the best man. My buddy and his fiancée thought it would be good for Liz and I to meet before the wedding, so they set up a dinner for just the four of us. I say it was *sort of* a blind date because Liz had been on-again, off-again with someone and since she was on-again with him at the time we weren't really considering it a *date*. But that was what it ended up seeming like when we hit it off."

"A blind date that worked out?"

"I guess that depends on how you look at it since it led to marriage but then divorce."

"Was she the reason you went to Detroit after you got out of the service?"

"She was certainly a factor. My army buddy and his wife were from Detroit, too. They encouraged me to relocate rather than come back to Northbridge. Northbridge did seem pretty isolated after being out in the world, and with Liz in Detroit, too? When Jack and I were discharged and that's where he went, I decided to tag along."

Eden thought he was downplaying his attraction to his former wife and she told him so.

"I definitely wanted to see if we had a chance," he admitted. "But remember, she was involved with someone else."

"Did you break them up?"

"No," he said as if that were an insult. "Liz had let the other guy know we'd met, that we liked each other, that she was having misgivings about him and wanted to explore things with me. She expected that to end her relationship with the other guy but he hung on and said if she needed to date me for a while to get it out of her system, she could see us both."

"How did you like that?"

He shrugged. "It wasn't as if I was ready for instant commitment, so I was okay with it." He smiled wryly. "And there was the challenge and competition that probably whetted my appetite a little more. Plus I'd joined the police force as soon as I got to Detroit and I was training and busy and trying to settle in. I didn't have a lot of time to sit around and twiddle my thumbs if she wasn't with me."

"How long did the dual-dating thing go on?"

"About a year. Then she called it quits with the other guy and we got serious."

Eden found it easy to understand how meeting Cam could jeopardize an unstable relationship, but difficult to understand it taking a whole year for the other woman to decide between someone else and Cam.

"And then you got married," Eden said.

"At the end of the second year. Even though she'd already started to have some problems with my being a cop."

Eden recalled the offhand comments he'd made before, apparently referring to that. "She didn't like it?"

"At first she didn't like it. Then she hated it."

There were obviously residual emotions when it came to his ex-wife because his expression was so tight a vein had appeared in his right temple.

"Everything you said last night about being a cop's wife," he continued, "was how Liz felt. Only magnified about a hundredfold. She said that if I was on duty her heart stopped every time she heard a siren—she actually had to start taking antianxiety drugs because the sound made her hyperventilate and throw up. If I was on grave-yard shift, she couldn't close her eyes all night. She wanted me to call her every hour, on the hour, so she'd know I was okay and if I didn't, if I was fifteen minutes late, she was sure I was dead and was calling the precinct, demanding information. I can see how you were freaked-out because you knew too much, but Liz was convinced the job was even more dangerous than it was and nothing I said could change her mind."

"I wasn't anywhere near that bad," Eden conceded. "Was she a worrier about other things, too, or just the job?"

"Other things, too. Before we got married I knew

she fretted a lot about things that seemed inconsequential to me, but I didn't know that her fretting was a sign that she didn't have a lot of perspective on anything. To Liz a headache was always a brain tumor, a bruise was potential leukemia, a mouse in the house was an infestation—everything was bigger to her than it actually was. But the job was definitely the worst and that was where her primary focus was once we'd made it through the wedding."

"That must have been rough on you both."

"And on the marriage," he said. "Especially since she wanted me to quit and I wouldn't do it."

Eden couldn't tell whether or not he regretted that he hadn't done what his ex-wife wanted. "If you had it to do over again, would you have quit?"

"Eventually I did."

He hadn't given her that impression. "Oh."

"Just not for the first two years of the marriage. Then Liz got pregnant. And I got shot."

Eden felt her eyebrows take a jump for her hairline. He'd been *shot* and his wife had been pregnant? Did he have a child somewhere?

That thought and the possibility that he might have kept it under wraps until now was very unnerving.

Eden reached for another mint and as she sat back again she repeated what she was still trying to get her mind around. "Your wife got pregnant and you got shot?"

Something about the way she'd said it made him smile but only slightly. "Well, not on the same day," he said. "Liz got pregnant and I got shot when she was about five months along. My partner and I answered a robbery-in-progress call at a liquor store. The perp had a gun and thought he'd try shooting his way out. I took a bullet in the thigh."

"That couldn't have eased your wife's mind," Eden said to prompt him.

"Definitely not. She was even more of a wreck after she found out she was pregnant anyway. She had all kinds of health issues then that her doctor said were stress related. She couldn't sleep even when I *was* home because she was so afraid something was going to happen to me. Her blood pressure spiked. She had more than just morning sickness—she couldn't keep food down most of the time, so there were weight issues.... Like I said, she was a wreck."

"And you still didn't consider quitting the force?"

"Sure, I considered it. But I really liked being a cop and I was good at it. There wasn't anything else I wanted to do—which I suppose was selfish. But I had Liz going to counseling, to wives' support groups—I made sure to let her know just how much of the job was routine and not dangerous at all, I even took her on a drive-along. I reassured her constantly that I was doing everything by the book. That I *wasn't* a first-one-through-the-door cop. I wore the vest. I was doing all I could to get her to relax and I just kept hoping that she would."

"And then you got shot."

"And then I got shot."

"In the leg, where wearing the vest didn't help."

"Right."

"How badly were you hurt?" Eden asked quietly.

"It wasn't good but it could have been worse. The bullet missed the femur and the femoral artery but it didn't just graze me. I had to have surgery and I was on crutches for a while. But I made a full recovery."

There certainly weren't any indications of anything to contradict that in what she'd seen of him on the basketball court tonight.

"Still, I'm guessing getting shot was enough to put your wife over the edge," Eden said.

Cam made a face that looked like a recoil. "Completely over the edge. It was bad. She collapsed at the hospital and ended up being admitted right along with me. She was so upset her doctors wanted to keep an eye on her to make sure she didn't go into labor or something. She didn't, but after that she gave me an ultimatum—the job, or her and the baby."

His own voice was quiet as he said that, letting her know how difficult that ultimatum had been for him.

Then he shrugged again to minimize it and said, "So once I'd recuperated enough to work again I got a job with a security company giving safety seminars and selling equipment and security alarms."

Eden could tell he hadn't been happy at that but she said, "Obviously it wasn't enough to save the marriage because here you are."

He laughed a humorless laugh. "No, it wasn't the solution. It helped make the rest of the pregnancy uneventful but not even that mattered." He paused and Eden saw the struggle it was for him to say what he said next. "The baby was stillborn."

Oh, that was much worse than the possibility that he had a child he hadn't told her about.

"I'm sorry," she said, not only in condolence but also because she felt awful that she'd used paying off a silly bet to initiate a conversation that was so serious and so painful. A conversation he might not have wanted to have. "I had no idea…."

He took a deep breath and let it out in a long, measured exhale. "Liz was convinced that the stress she'd been under before I quit the force had caused the baby's death. The doctors didn't think so but…" He shook his head and Eden saw the raw guilt he carried. "I don't know," he said. "What I do know is that the marriage hadn't been on steady ground before that and afterward…" He shook his head again. "Afterward things were even rockier. Too rocky to recover from. We were divorced eight months later."

"I shouldn't have made you get into all of this," Eden said.

"Nah, it's okay."

Still, she gave him a moment to regroup. When he had, he said, "I stayed in Detroit until the dust had settled but being a cop was still what I wanted to do. Only being a cop in Detroit again just didn't appeal to me. By then I was ready for… " He shrugged once more. "I don't know, I guess I was ready for a mellower way to do it. So I came back to Northbridge, got on the force, and here I am."

Eden nodded. She wasn't sure what to say now that he'd finished telling her what she'd basically coerced him into revealing. She also didn't know exactly how to lighten the mood, she only knew she wanted to.

"Okay, you win. You can keep all the rest of the cookies," she finally said.

Cam chuckled, his forehead furrowed with confusion. "Why?"

"Because I shouldn't have been so nosy and forced you to get into things that aren't any of my business just because I barely beat you at a dumb game of pool."

"Hey, I'm just glad you're admitting that it was *barely*," he said, clearly using the opening she'd given him to put the subject of his own tragic past behind them.

"Barely, but I *did* beat you," she countered to keep the lighter vein going.

"You're determined to kill my buzz tonight, aren't you?"

Eden laughed. "Your chocolate chip cookie buzz?"

"It started long before the cookie high," he said, his dark blue eyes steady and intent on her face.

"A basketball buzz?" she inquired more flirtatiously than she'd realized she was going to.

"I think the buzz started initially when I saw you coming into the gym tonight."

"Oh, I don't believe that!" she joked.

"It's true. And then the buzz grew with every glimpse I got of you at Adz. Especially of you bending over that pool table…." He seemed to savor that image for a split second. "That's what did me in."

"Liar," she teasingly accused, pretending not to notice that the hand that had been near her shoulder on the back sofa cushion had reached to play with the spray of curls at her crown. "If seeing me at Adz was giving you a buzz you wouldn't have kept your distance."

"That's *why* I was keeping my distance. Imagine getting a buzz from somebody you know doesn't really want anything to do with you."

"Who said I don't want anything to do with you?" she asked, quick to disabuse him of that notion.

"You *do* want something to do with me?" he challenged.

Admitting that was risky. Even just admitting it to herself. The closest she would go was, "Let's say things would be a lot less complicated for me if I *didn't* want anything to do with you."

"Mmm," he muttered as if he knew exactly what she meant because he felt the same way.

And then that hand that had been playing with her hair came to the side of her face in a whisper of a caress as his eyes held hers and his oh-so-handsome face moved closer and closer....

Maybe she shouldn't have made him forbidden fruit, she told herself as his mouth met hers. Because forbidden fruit was just so irresistible.

And she couldn't resist him. She didn't. She accepted a kiss that began softly, slowly, tentatively. She returned it. And when his lips parted, when he took the kiss to the next level, she went along without hesitation. She parted her lips, too. She let her head fall back just a little to accommodate him. She even raised her own hand to his chest and drank in the feel of his hard pectorals beneath his sweater.

He's a cop, she reminded herself, hoping that would stall things. *He's a cop who will always be a cop.*

But at that moment it didn't make any difference to her. At that moment he wasn't a cop. He was Cam. He was the drop-dead gorgeous, sexy, hunk of a man who haunted her dreams and almost all of her waking thoughts. He was the guy she longed to be with when she wasn't and relished every minute of when she was. He was the one person she was so hot for that nothing she told herself right then mattered as much as that kiss and the fact that he *was* kissing her again, that last night hadn't been the end. Even if it should have been…

His other arm circled her waist and repositioned her so she was leaning back against the couch as he came nearer, pressing her slightly into the cushions. Both of her arms went around him, her hands splayed against his mighty back, bringing her breasts in joyful contact with him. Her nipples went instantly hard and while she had no idea if he knew, she was so aware of the need they were relaying that she had to work at not arching her back to more insistently poke him with them.

The kiss deepened yet again, mouths opened wider and his tongue became an instrument of delight, taunting hers to frolic, dominating and submitting in turns, circling, seeking, even luring hers to follow into his own sweet, minty depths.

Her head was completely braced on the sofa by then as one of Cam's arms was curved above it, his fingers toying with her hair once more. His other hand was on her side, doing a sensual massage that was setting things alight in her so intensely that her breasts seemed to be straining for him all on their own, achingly in need of his attention and turning her thoughts to his bare skin.

Craving the feel of it, she slipped her hands under the bottom of his sweater and coursed upward again, filling both palms with the warm expanse of sleek masculine skin over solid muscle.

She hadn't meant for that to be an invitation for him to follow suit. Or maybe, subconsciously, she had. But either way, that must have been how he took it because that hand at her side found the hem of her own shirts and slipped underneath.

That big, powerful, slightly callused hand laid gently on her rib cage, continuing the massage with an even more sensual bent that made her blood rush faster through her veins, that made her almost crazy with the need to feel that hand on more than merely her side.

She took a deep breath that pressed her breasts into him and whether he read that as a signal or not, that talented hand finally began to move leisurely upward....

Yes! Keep going! she was shouting in her mind as her mouth opened even wider beneath his and that kiss became a soul-searching, uninhibited plundering that was nearing frenzy stage when his hand reached her breast. But only over her bra, making her hate that bit of lace that had cost her more than it could ever be worth.

Apparently Cam wasn't any happier about the barrier than she was because he didn't waste much time before he slipped the half cup down and freed that smallish globe of yearning into the heat of his palm.

Eden tightened her throat to keep from moaning at that first contact. And if she'd thought his hand on her bare side had felt good, it was nothing compared to the way he touched her breast. Which was why, even though she managed not to make any noises, she couldn't refrain from arching her spine and nudging the taut kernel of her nipple into the innermost hollow of his palm.

He closed around her straining flesh, working it like a fragile mound of clay, kneading, lifting, pressing into it. Then he located that tightly knotted crest with his fingertips, tugging, tweaking, pinching, rolling it with careful tenderness and heightening her pleasure with each touch, each tease, each delicious torment.

Eden raised her hands higher on his naked back, bringing his sweater up with them, thinking she might sweep it over his head and toss it aside so she could have full and free rein over his torso. So she could finally see his chest, his broad shoulders, his biceps without even the scant coverage of the T-shirts he'd had on tonight and that other night when she'd watched him work out in the room above the garage. So that maybe he might rid her of her top, too, and she could have her breasts pressed to that chest she knew had to be amazing….

But even as that idea enticed her, something else went through her mind—where would they go from here? Where would they go once clothing had actually been removed?

And while Cam being a cop hadn't been enough to stall the onset of this, the thought of where discarded clothing would lead gave her pause.

Where *would* they go once shirts had actually been taken off?

Maybe somewhere she wasn't sure she was ready to go. Somewhere she was sure she *shouldn't go.* No matter how wonderful it was to kiss him like this or to have his big body above hers or his hand on her eager breast.

And it *was* wonderful. Astonishingly wonderful…

But what about when it's over? a little voice in the back of her mind asked.

And because she didn't have an answer, she knew this had gone as far as it could.

She took her hands out from under his sweater,

grabbed the hem of it and the T-shirt that was caught in its folds and pulled them both down.

It was enough of a message for their kiss to calm, for his hand at her breast to pause, for him to put just a hint of space between them. And into that space Eden raised her hands to his chest again, this time to push ever so lightly.

And that really was message enough.

Cam slipped his hand out from under her top and that plundering kiss became something almost chaste before he ended that, too.

He gazed into her eyes and smiled a sheepish smile. "Look at where sharing cookies can lead," he joked.

"Maybe the special ingredient that wins Marge Baxter awards is some kind of aphrodisiac."

"Maybe," he said with a laugh.

Then he moved away from her and Eden sat up straight, weak with wanting him right back where he'd been before.

"I just..." She tried to come up with a coherent reason for why she'd stopped him.

"Yeah, I know," he said to what she hadn't found words for, letting her know he had misgivings of his own that he couldn't voice, either.

"It's late and I probably better get going anyway," he added. "We have the age progressions to do again tomorrow."

Eden had forgotten about that.

"That's right," she said, hating that she sounded so foggy. But it was the best she could do while more than half of her brain was still thinking about him and that great body and how good it felt to have him touch her....

Cam stood and put on his coat. "I'm off duty this

weekend but I'll go in for this. So there's no sense taking two cars. Why don't I pick you up?"

"Okay," she said, still trying to get a grip on herself.

"But since it's Saturday and we shouldn't have to go in, let's give ourselves the morning off at least. How about we leave around one?"

"One is good," Eden confirmed.

She stood, too, to walk him to the door, remembering the remaining cookies half way there.

"Oh, the cookies! Take them with you," she said, returning to the living room for the box.

Cam didn't refuse them but even as he accepted the pink bakery box when she met him at the front door and handed it to him, Eden didn't have the impression he was thinking about that. His eyes were too steadfastly on hers, delving into them as if they held the answers to mysteries. Although to what mysteries she didn't know.

After a moment he smiled, though, and said, "This all might be easier if you'd just stuck with the glasses and the braces and the frizzy hair."

"Or if you could just be a jerk," she countered in the same humorous vein.

"Shall we work on that?" he asked with a hint of a forlorn crinkle between his beautiful blue eyes.

But she didn't *want* him to be a jerk. She liked him too much the way he was. So she said, "Maybe we should just work on some restraint."

He nodded his agreement but he said, "That hasn't been too successful so far."

"I know," she whispered.

"We'll try harder?" he queried without much conviction.

"And not eat any more cookies spiked with aphrodisiac," she joked, unsure if she could ever succeed at restraining what seemed to be set loose in her each time she was with him.

He made no move to leave, studying her face, still smiling that small smile that told her nothing. Then he leaned forward and kissed her again, softly, briefly and yet with lips parted enough to let her know what had started on the couch was still simmering beneath the surface.

"Tomorrow. One," he said when he ended the kiss and straightened up again.

"Tomorrow at one," Eden repeated.

Cam opened the door and went outside, offering only a raise of his chin to say good-night.

As Eden stood there watching him go, she wrapped her arms around her middle, hugging herself tight as if against the cold.

But the truth was, she was just doing all she could to retain some control.

Otherwise she might have given in to what was still throbbing inside of her.

She might have given in to wanting him in the worst way and begged him to come back....

Chapter Ten

Eden was not in top form Saturday afternoon at the police station. Not with Cam right there beside her at the computer.

He looked great in a cream-colored Henley sweater and a pair of jeans that highlighted the supreme derriere they encased. He was clean-shaven, he smelled terrific, and combined with the way the evening before had ended and the unsatisfied desire that she'd been left with, she just wasn't herself.

At the best of times, her response to him was primitive and barely containable. But that afternoon it was on overdrive. And despite what she knew intellectually, despite what she tried to do to block the response or keep it from happening, it happened anyway. Clouding her thinking. Slowing her reflexes. And certainly diminishing her job performance. Basically, she was all thumbs—she kept hitting the wrong keys on the keyboard, messing up the commands she logged into the computer, calling upon the wrong functions. And as a result she had to redo things three and four times before she got them right.

But finally, late in the day, she settled on an image that made Cam sit back in his chair and say, "I was beginning to think this was where you were headed. I know who that is."

He said that as if it were the last thing he ever wanted to admit and Eden sat back, as well, to give herself a better view. "She looks familiar to me, too, but I can't place her."

"Leslie. That's Leslie Vance," he said in amazement.

"I've been away a long time—remind me who Leslie Vance is."

"She's…" Cam shook his head. "She's worked at my family's dry cleaners since before I was born. When my mother was alive, Leslie was her best friend."

"The lady at the dry cleaners," Eden reiterated as it dawned on her. "Is that really my *grandmother?*"

"Your grandmother and someone who's been like a member of my family my entire life."

"Honestly? And I hardly even remember her," Eden marveled, staring at the computer screen.

"Probably because Leslie has always stayed in the background. Quiet, unassuming, unobtrusive Leslie— we thought she was just pathologically shy and that the only reason she was comfortable with us was because of Mom. Because they were friends and worked side by side every day. The way Leslie has with my sister since Mara took over the cleaners." He shook his head again.

"Geez, I can't believe this and Mara...Mara is going to freak out."

He and his family had clearly had more contact with her grandmother than Eden had and it seemed even harder for him to accept that the woman who had been Leslie to all of Northbridge for decades was really Celeste Perry.

"Do you think your mother knew the truth?" Eden asked him, baffled by all of this.

"I'm sure she didn't, no. My mother wasn't originally from Northbridge. She was born in Washington State to parents who thought they couldn't have kids. She was the midlife baby and she was barely out of her teens when they both died. They left her a little money and she came here and bought the dry cleaners. But that was in 1969 and by then the bank robbery was old news."

"So she wouldn't have met Celeste when she was Celeste."

"Right. Mom said that Leslie—Celeste—just showed up one day at the cleaners. Mom had a Help Wanted sign in the window, Leslie applied for the job and Mom hired her. They worked together every day, and they became friends even though Leslie was almost ten years older than Mom."

"Best friends," Eden reminded him, trying to get as clear a picture as she could of the course her grandmother had followed when she'd returned to Northbridge.

"Best friends," Cam confirmed. "Leslie went along when my mother eloped with my father, she was their witness. My mother said Leslie was the first person after her and my father to hold each one of us kids when we were born. She helped my mother through a near breakdown when my old man took off on us all. She came to every holiday dinner—and still does—because she didn't have anywhere else to go and Mom didn't want her to be by herself. She helped us take care of Mom when Mom got kidney disease and went into failure. Hell, Leslie was holding my mother's hand when Mom died...." He shook his head yet again and said, "I can't believe this."

"You never had a clue who she really was?"

"Never."

"What about my family? Did she talk about us? About Dad or Uncle Carl? About the Reverend?" Eden asked, trying to get a grip on the situation herself.

"No. I mean she never talked about any of you in a way that I ever remember standing out or seeming unusual."

"What about her past, before she went to work at the dry cleaners? She must have said something about that."

"She honestly didn't. Mom said Leslie was from all over, that her father had been in the military so she'd moved around a lot, but Leslie never talked about it to us. When she was with us, she was just..." He shrugged. "She was just with us—which is true to this day, now that I think about it. She asks how we are, what we're doing, if we're seeing anyone, that sort of thing. And I guess we ask her the same kinds of things."

"Small talk," Eden said.

"Sure. But you know how it is, when you've known someone all your life, you just sort of figure you know everything there is *to* know about them. Mom said Leslie had told her that Leslie's parents had died before she came to Northbridge, that she didn't have any other family. That she was all alone in the world. It was something my Mom said more than once when she was left on her own with seven kids to raise—she said that at least she had us, Leslie didn't have anyone. That Leslie only had us, too."

"So you—and the rest of your brothers and sisters— have been close to her."

"Yeah, but apparently it's been in a pretty selfish way since it's all always been about us and never about her."

"Isn't that how she would have needed it to be?"

"Sure, but…" More head shaking. "This is just so damn weird. I've been the one to keep saying what if Celeste has been right here under our noses all this time. But it never occurred to me that she could have been right under my own nose without my having the slightest inkling…."

Then he seemed to remember that they were talking about her flesh and blood, and he said, "I'm sorry. This has to be strange for you, too. Especially knowing that your own grandmother lived in Northbridge—within blocks of where you grew up—and you didn't even know her. Did Leslie—Celeste—ever approach you? Or your dad or your uncle, that you know of?"

Eden shook her head, once more studying the image she'd generated to reveal the woman who had kept her identity a secret. "She never approached me, no. She was just the woman who worked at the dry cleaners. The most I ever said to her was to ask if she could remove a stain from a party dress of my mother's. I don't know if anyone else in the family had much to do with her. I've never heard my dad or my uncle or my sisters or my cousins mention her in any special way."

"I know she kept to herself with the exception of her

friendship with my mother and being with us as a result of that. My mother said she'd tried to get Leslie to date early on but that Leslie wasn't interested, and even when it came to town events Mom had to twist Leslie's arm to get her to go even occasionally. Since Mom's death Mara has tried to get her not to be so reclusive but she hasn't had much luck, either. Shy—like I said, we've always written off Leslie's lack of socializing to shyness."

"And yet she worked the counter at the dry cleaners where everyone in town saw her at one time or another."

"Hiding in plain sight?" Cam guessed. "Or courting disaster? I can't explain it."

"I'd say hiding in plain sight. She had to support herself so she took the job but she was probably afraid that the more exposure she got, the more chance there would be of someone recognizing her, so she didn't do much else."

"I don't think there was a high risk of anyone recognizing her," Cam said, holding up the old newspaper photograph of Celeste Perry next to the picture on the computer screen to prove his point.

In the photograph of her at twenty-two she was very thin with wavy, pale blond hair and a pretty, unlined face. In Eden's initial images there had been a resemblance to that. But since Eden had made the changes the waitress in Bozeman had suggested, the age progression was much different. Eden had added enough weight to take Celeste from matronly to obese. She'd included deeper lines from beside her nose down to the corners of her mouth, giving Celeste a sort of sadness. She'd changed the hair from the nondescript, grayish-toned granny cut a seventy-three-year-old woman might wear to the coal-black, tight bun that the waitress had most recently described. The end result was that there was only the most scant resemblance between the Celeste of the 1950's and the Leslie Vance that Northbridge knew.

And the longer Eden stared at the image of the woman who was her grandmother, the more she regretted that she'd done the age progression. She hadn't expected to feel guilty. She'd never felt that way before, when her sculptures or computer work had been instrumental in the recognition and arrest of anyone.

But somehow this was different. Whether because Leslie Vance was someone she knew—however vaguely—or because there *was* a blood connection, she didn't know. But she felt sad to have been the one to expose a woman who had lived an almost secluded life in the small town she'd run away from. A woman who, after that rash act, had apparently wanted badly enough to be back here to accept a life barely lived if it could be lived in Northbridge, near the family she'd abandoned. A woman who had been a good friend to Cam's family. And now, years and years later, her true identity would be publicly aired and it was anybody's guess what would happen to her.

All because of Eden.

She thought that for the first time she agreed with her grandfather—she shouldn't have done the computer imaging.

"Maybe we should just keep this between the two of us," she suggested.

Cam didn't answer for so long that she knew he was seriously considering it.

But then he shook his head once again, slowly and

with resignation. "You know we can't do that. There are records now, other people who know the Bozeman waitress gave us more information, that we were going to change what you came up with earlier this week."

"What if I change it some other way?"

Cam smiled sympathetically. "The weight and the hair are definites and they're the giveaways."

"We could warn Leslie—Celeste—and let her leave town before we show this to anyone. Give her the opportunity to run."

"That would make us accessories, Eden. To a possible murder."

"You think she killed the second robber?"

"No, I don't. Especially not now that I know who she is," Cam answered.

"But you think she could be tried for it." The possibility sent a chill up Eden's spine.

"I don't know," Cam said. "I don't know how this is going to play out. And we won't know where it might go until we talk to Leslie. Until we hear what she has to say."

"*We?* You and I? Could we go and see her before everyone else barges in? Before the FBI and the state cops swarm all over her? Can we at least let her prepare for it?" It wasn't much, but it was something Eden discovered, only in that instant, that she wanted to do.

"I meant *we* as in the police and the FBI," he qualified.

But still he seemed to be considering her request.

Then, whether or not it was protocol, Eden had the impression that he was giving in to his own emotional entanglements with Celeste.

"I'm going to have to notify everyone else, but it'll

take some time for them to get here. And before they do, yeah, let's you and I go talk to Leslie."

"Cameron, honey, what a nice surprise!"

Under other circumstances Eden might have smiled at the sound of Cam's full name used by the woman she'd known as Leslie Vance until an hour ago. But as it was, Eden couldn't find any humor in it when the older woman opened her apartment door to them.

"And Eden Perry! I'd heard you were back in town. How wonderful to—"

"Les, this isn't a social call," Cam said, cutting her off, maybe because her pleasure at seeing them was as painful for him as it was for Eden.

The apartment that was over the dry cleaners was also owned by the Pratt family. Leslie had lived there for as long as she'd worked for the Pratts, and now she took a step out of the doorway that faced an alley behind the building. Her very round face had sobered but she didn't appear alarmed. Instead she merely looked calmly resigned.

"Come on in," she invited.

Cam waited for Eden to accept the invitation before he took up the rear and closed the door behind them.

It was the first time Eden had ever been in Leslie's home and it struck her all the more just how odd and unsettling this whole thing was.

This woman is my grandmother, she kept telling herself as she glanced around the small apartment that was sedately but tastefully decorated.

"Please sit," the older woman said as she lowered her ungainly body into a large armchair.

Eden and Cam sat on the love seat across from her.

Once they had, Cam said, "We know you're Celeste Perry, Les."

She nodded serenely. "Armand finally told, didn't he?"

"The Reverend?" Cam said in surprise. "He knew?"

The older woman merely smiled, offering no answer. Instead she said, "How did you find out then?"

"It's my fault," Eden blurted out.

"Because of that computer thingy you do?" the older woman said. "I've seen the picture—we have one in the window downstairs. But it doesn't look anything like me."

"We changed it this afternoon according to some things a waitress in Bozeman told us," Cam offered.

"Oh, I'll bet you're talking about Carmin. I worked in a diner in Bozeman with Carmin. She was a blabbermouth. I guess some things never change."

Cam handed her the printout of the revised picture.

The woman known as Leslie Vance glanced at it and nodded. "Yes, that looks much more like me. You did a good job, Eden," she said with pride.

"I'm sorry," Eden said, knowing it probably sounded ridiculous but needing to apologize anyway.

"It's all right," her grandmother assured. "I've known since they found the duffel bag at the bridge that this was going to happen. It's almost a relief that it finally has."

"I've had to report to the state police and to the FBI," Cam said. "As of now you aren't under formal arrest but any minute a state patrolman will be coming to keep you under watch to make sure you don't go anywhere."

"Cam refused to arrest you and bring you into jail to hold you for questioning even though that's what the other authorities wanted him to do," Eden explained because she thought her grandmother should know about the fight he'd put up for Celeste before they'd arrived at her apartment. "He convinced them that there's not enough evidence to base an arrest on at this point and the most he would agree to was that a guard be posted outside so you don't disappear."

"Thank you, Cameron. You're a good boy."

That seemed to embarrass him because he cleared his throat and fidgeted slightly before he said, "I'm going to read you your rights anyway, Les—" He cut himself short. "Or would you rather I call you Celeste?"

"Celeste, please. If you don't mind. It's funny, but even after all these years of using that name, it's just never felt like me."

"Celeste," he said, trying it out. Then he continued. "I'm going to read you your rights because I had to agree to that, at least. The state cops don't want any legal loopholes."

Cam did read her her Miranda rights but Celeste didn't seem interested. Instead, as he did, she studied Eden as if, for the first time, she could look at her the way she wanted to—openly and without censoring herself.

When Cam had finished, Celeste said to Eden, "You're so beautiful. You've always reminded me of my Momma. She had those same ice-blue eyes and she was bookish, like you. She told me she was all elbows and knees as a girl, too, the way you were growing up. But, like you, she turned from the ugly duckling into the swan."

So Celeste had watched her closely enough to know she'd been an ugly duckling….

Before Eden had thanked her for the compliment, her grandmother went on. "I was so sorry to hear about your husband. I went in to Billings one day when I'd heard you were bringing him to meet your folks and I sneaked a peek at him—"

"You went all the way to Billings just because you'd heard I was going to bring Alika there?"

"Oh, I went any number of times. I have since Jack and Carl moved there. To see them, even if they didn't know I was there. And every time I found out you'd be visiting them I had to go for sure. Since you didn't come back to Northbridge it was the only way."

The sadness Eden had felt earlier grew at the thought of this woman going to such pains just for a glimpse of people who barely knew she existed. People who she clearly thought of and cared for.

"Anyhow," Celeste continued, "I got to see your husband that one time. He was such a strapping man and you seemed so in love with him. It must have been unbearable to lose him."

"It was no fun," Eden understated. But at that moment her own grief seemed secondary to what was going on.

Celeste returned her focus to Cam. "I suppose you want to know my whole sordid story, don't you?"

"I do," he confessed. "But I won't let you tell it right now. You need a lawyer. And I want you to promise me that you won't say anything until you've been counseled and have that lawyer by your side."

Celeste made a face, dismissing that idea. "My greatest sin was against Armand and my sons, Cameron."

"That may be true—"

"There's no *maybe* about it. It is true. I wronged Armand right from the start. Like your mom, I lost my parents when I was very young. I didn't have any other family, I was at terrible loose ends, and that's when I met Armand. He was so sure of himself, of who he was, what he wanted, where he was going in life. Being with him made me feel safe and so I married him. But I didn't love him."

"Please don't say any more," Cam beseeched. "If it comes to a trial, both Eden and I could be called to testify about whatever you tell us now."

"I won't tell you about that other stuff, if it bothers you. But I want you—" she looked to Eden, as well "—I want you both to know what was behind what I did. How I came to it. Surely none of *that* can be used against me."

"You never know, Les...Celeste. Better to be safe than sorry."

Celeste waved away that notion and went on in spite of Cam's warnings.

"I thought that I would eventually learn to love Armand. That we would get closer and from that, passion would naturally happen. But back then Armand was just as he is now—not a warm man. Not someone who allows for much closeness even with people he should be close to. So, sadly, I never fell in love with him. I never felt passion for him. And maybe if Carl and Jack hadn't come along so soon, I might not have stayed with Armand for as long as I did."

"But right away you had two kids, eleven months apart," Eden said.

"One baby only ten months after the wedding and yes, the second just eleven months later," Celeste confirmed. "But I did love them," she was quick to add. "With all my heart. They were my babies...."

Celeste's eyes grew moist but she fought the tears.

"I wasn't the best mother, though," she said after a moment. "I tried. Truly. And I wanted to be a good mother to them. But I was scatterbrained in those days. It was Armand who had to tell me when they should be weaned and toilet trained and how to do it. It was Armand who made sure I didn't give them too many cookies or too much candy when I wanted to do that to make them happy. It was Armand who had to tell me what to do when one of the boys fell and cut his head or skinned his knees. Armand who had to be the disciplinarian because I would cry when he spanked one of them or sent them to their room."

"My dad said that from what he remembered of you, you were the fun parent," Eden offered, omitting the fact that she knew how strict, stringent, demanding, critical and tyrannical her grandfather was, and that her father had missed the tempering influence of his mother when she'd left.

"Anyway," Celeste continued. "a passionless marriage is not an easy thing to stick with year after year. And while Armand was a fine, upstanding, moral man, he was very cold and after several years of that...I wanted more," she admitted reluctantly. "And less, too, to be honest."

"You wanted more *and* less?" Cam asked.

"I wanted more life. More passion. More excitement. More fun. And less of what it meant to be the Reverend's wife."

"Especially in a small town," Cam guessed.

"Yes. There are a lot of pressures and demands on the wife of a clergyman," Celeste said as if the mere thought of it exhausted and overwhelmed her. "And because

Armand was that clergyman and the sort of person he was on top of it…" She sighed. "Well, I had to be perfect. And believe me, I'm not—never was and never will be. And I was young, with two small children on top of needing to oversee church functions outside of the services and… Well, I just wasn't up to it all. Especially not when there was nothing from Armand to help ease the load. From Armand there were just more pressures and demands and expectations. And the constant berating over why I couldn't live up to his standards—"

Celeste cut herself off, sighed and shrugged. "And about the time I thought I just couldn't take it anymore, Mickey Rider and Frank Dorian came to town."

"That's where you need to stop, Celeste," Cam ordered.

"I know, I'll be careful. But you both have to understand," the older woman insisted, "it wasn't easy for me to leave my babies. But when I decided that was what I was going to do, I felt my boys would be better off with the parent who knew all the answers. I just didn't realize it would hurt so badly or do what it did to me to leave them behind. I guess you could say I'm wearing the proof of how awful I felt because when I'm upset I eat and, well, you can see for yourself how upset I was. I was just so sorry for leaving my sons. I knew I'd ruined my life and I was miserable. Then I found myself alone and penniless in Alaska—"

"Careful what you say," Cam cautioned again.

Celeste nodded. "I knew then that there was only a single thing I really wanted—to get back to where I could be near Carl and Jack. Of course I was sure I couldn't ever just go home and be a mother to my boys again, but just to be somewhere close to them, to at least know how they were, what they were doing, maybe even to see them again…."

There was such longing in her voice and in her expression, it was evident how deeply she'd wanted to be near her children.

"So," she continued, "I worked any job I could get—waiting tables, cleaning, factory work, and whenever I could get the money together I'd buy a bus ticket to anywhere that would bring me in this direction. Once I got back to Montana I moved in a kind of circle around Northbridge—Bozeman, Livingston, Laurel, Red Lodge, Hardin, Forsyth, Miles City, just to name a few. I would work for a while, save my money, and just live for when I could quietly get hold of a Northbridge newspaper and hope there was anything in it about the boys…." Her voice cracked and it was obvious she was struggling with a new bout of tears. "I just missed them so much I can't even begin to tell you."

"How did you end up getting back here?" Eden asked.

"It took a good look in the mirror," she said with some self-deprecating humor. "I'd gone along, just trying to survive, depressed, lonely, in the depths of despair. Certainly the last thing I'd cared about or paid any attention to was my appearance. And suddenly I couldn't believe what I saw. I didn't look anything like I had. I'd aged—I guess from the stress and strain and because I hadn't taken care of myself. And the weight had crept up to where I am now. Frank had had me dye my hair black as a disguise before he'd even left me in Alaska and I'd kept it that way. And there just wasn't a glimmer of my old self in what was looking back at me. I started to think that if even *I* didn't recognize me, maybe no one else would, either. That was when I made my first trip here. I was so scared I think I shook throughout the day I spent in town, but by the end of it, when no one had known who I was, I got brave and decided to try moving back as someone else."

"Leslie Vance," Cam said.

"Leslie Vance," she repeated.

"And that was when you went to work at the dry cleaners?" Eden asked.

"That was when. Cameron's mom owned it and she let me rent this place, too. And I've been here ever since."

Celeste smiled another small smile, this one melancholy. "It might have been from a distance, but I've been able to see my boys get married, to see my grandbabies grow up, to know what's going on with you all. And even if it wasn't much, it was still more than I had for those awful years after I left Armand."

"And has the Reverend known it was you all along?" Cam asked, returning to the question she'd left unanswered earlier.

Again Celeste seemed hesitant to respond.

But after a moment she said, "I'd been here about two years before he recognized me. And even then it wasn't from the way I look. He came into the dry cleaners to pick up some things and I slipped and called him by name. Something about that and the way I said it was what got me caught."

"But he kept your secret?" Eden asked.

"I wasn't sure he would. I think he genuinely hates me. He stormed out that day and for two more days I expected the police to show up any second to arrest me. But instead, on the third day, Armand came back to the

cleaners when I was there alone. He said he'd thought
about it and if I stayed away from him and his family,
if I never let anyone know I had any connection to any
of you, if I did nothing but look on the way anyone else
in town who had no business with you all did, he
wouldn't go to the police. He said he didn't want any
more embarrassment and humiliation, and it would
serve as my punishment to be kept to the sidelines
around our family. I promised that was what I'd do and
it's what I've done. And he's never spoken to me since."

The elderly woman had gone from sitting up straight
in her chair to slumping there as if every ounce of energy
had suddenly been drained from her.

Eden saw it and said, "Maybe you should rest now."

"You know, I think that might be best," Celeste
conceded. "Besides," she added with an amused glance
at Cam, "I don't think poor Cameron can take any more
worry that I'll say something I shouldn't."

"I can't," he acknowledged.

But he didn't leap to his feet. Instead he said, "Will
you be all right alone or would you like me to stay? We
can play cards or a game or something that doesn't
involve talking."

"Oh, no, dear, I don't need my hand held. I've gotten
used to being alone after all these years. I think I'll have
a stiff drink and go to bed. Eden is right, I need some
rest. Especially since I'm sure the worst is to come."

Eden wished they could refute that but they couldn't,
not with interrogations from the state police and the
FBI looming ahead for Celeste.

Cam did stand then, going to the apartment window
beside the door.

"There's a State Patrol car down there," he announced after a glance outside. "I'll have a talk with the patrolman. He won't bother you. Unless you try to go anywhere."

"I won't," Celeste said wearily.

Eden stood then, too, but Celeste didn't get up to see them to the door and Eden thought it was an indication of just how worn-out the older woman was.

"I'll check back with you," Eden told her.

That brought a genuine smile to the round face and, on what seemed like an impulse, Celeste reached for her hand, taking it and squeezing it. "I'd like that so much. I'm sorry for all this. And for deceiving you, Eden. But if I hadn't Armand would have turned me in and everything would have blown up long before now."

"I understand. You did what you had to do under the circumstances," Eden said, squeezing the puffy hand in return. "You're sure you'll be okay?"

"Positive," Celeste assured, releasing her grip to let her go.

Eden didn't rush to leave, though, wondering if she should insist on staying. But that seemed strange, too, when—blood relatives or not—they didn't actually know each other.

So in the end she decided it might be best if she respected the other woman's wishes to be left on her own.

Cam must have seen her dilemma and realized that she needed a little assistance getting to the door, because he opened it expectantly and said, "We'll let you have that drink and get to bed, Celeste. But if you need anything, call me. Middle of the night or not."

"I will."

"I don't think anybody will be here to question you

for a few days, maybe longer. They'll want to gather as much evidence against you as they can now that they know who you are. But I'll keep tabs on things and let you know what's going on."

"Thank you, Cameron. For everything," Celeste said yet again. "And Cameron? When it comes to talking about that night of the bank robbery? Armand was a witness to what went on down at the bridge."

Eden stopped short at that information and so did Cam.

"The Reverend has not only known who you really are for the last thirty-odd years, he was also a witness?" Cam repeated.

Celeste confirmed it with a nod of her head. "If only he'll speak up."

"He definitely hasn't been forthcoming up to this point," Cam said with a dark frown. "You're sure he was there? You saw him?"

"I saved his life," Celeste said matter-of-factly. "But I'll take your advice and keep that story to myself until I have a lawyer. You two go on now, go."

Eden didn't know what else to say and apparently neither did Cam, who stood at the door, looking dumbfounded.

Eden finally joined him there and he merely opened the apartment door and let her go out ahead of him.

"You're sure you'll be okay?" she heard him ask Celeste once more.

"Fine," Celeste answered.

Eden glanced over her shoulder and saw Cam nod before he closed the door.

For a moment they paused on the landing as that last bombshell sank in.

Then Eden said, "The Reverend has had information all this time and never said anything?"

Cam only answered with wide eyes and raised eyebrows before he ushered her down the stairs to the alley below.

The sight of the State Patrol car had a strong effect on Eden and brought a new, irrefutable message of just how severe the situation was.

Cam must have seen the effect it had on her because he took her arm, offering support.

"Come on," he said, bolstering her with the strength of his voice, as well. "Give me five minutes with this guy to make sure he knows not to bother her and then I'll take you home and pour you a good stiff drink, too."

Chapter Eleven

Eden waited in Cam's SUV, watching the snow that had begun to fall while he had a brief discussion with the State Patrolman in the alley behind Celeste Perry's apartment. Then they went to Eden's house.

Cam ordered Chinese food for dinner and kept his word about fixing her a strong drink—one of the best martinis she'd ever had. He also built a roaring fire in her fireplace and arranged an area for them to sit in front of it on the floor with a down quilt and the cushions and throw pillows from her sofa providing a backrest against the couch.

It was warm and cozy, the food and drink were just what Eden needed, Cam didn't bring up anything to do with her grandmother, and by midevening—with a full stomach and a slightly light head—Eden was finally starting to become comfortable with what the day had revealed.

They were sitting together on the quilt, Eden with her back to the cushions, Cam with his to the hearth, facing her. They both had their jeans-clad legs stretched out, snowy shoes removed, stockinged feet next to each other's hips. Cam had stopped drinking after one martini. Eden was nursing her second.

"How did your sister take the news that Leslie is really Celeste?" Eden asked, for the first time broaching the subject of her grandmother.

She was referring to the fact that Cam had decided on the drive back that beyond alerting his fellow officers, the one person who should know where the investigation had led was Mara. Of all the Pratts, he'd said, Mara was the most like a daughter to Celeste and he knew his sister would want to offer the older woman comfort and support. So he'd called his sister as soon as they'd gotten home.

"Mara reacted much like we did," he answered. "Stunned. There was such a long silence on the other end when I told her that I thought for a minute she might have passed out. Then she told me I was crazy, that it couldn't be. She didn't buy it until I said that Celeste didn't even try to deny it."

"It has to be even tougher to believe when Mara has worked with Celeste every day."

"I'm sure."

"Will she stand by Celeste the way you thought?"

"She was going to rush over to the apartment right then but I said Les—Celeste was going to bed. Mara will be there at the crack of dawn, though, I'm sure."

Eden was glad to hear that. It helped her to know that her grandmother wouldn't be abandoned by those who knew her best.

"Do you think Celeste is telling the truth about the Reverend?" she asked Cam then, finally feeling as if she could discuss what the older woman had told them.

"As Leslie, I've always known her to be an honest person. Except, I guess, for the fact that she *wasn't* Leslie. But in my experience, if someone says there was a witness, there was. Even if the witness denies it."

"And that's a mystery in itself, isn't it? Why—especially if Celeste saved his life—hasn't the Reverend ever stepped up and talked about what happened that night?"

Cam shrugged. "Experience has also taught me that if a witness refuses to *be* a witness, they have reasons of their own. Sometimes the reason is that they didn't see an incident quite the way it's being depicted by whoever's ass is on the line. But your questions are ones I'll be asking the Reverend when I talk to him."

"That won't be too soon, you know?" Eden said, setting aside her martini with only a sip or two remaining because she was getting a little drunk.

"No, I didn't know. Why won't I be able to see him anytime soon?" Cam asked.

"Eve took him to catch a bus out of town Friday night. That's why we were late getting to your basketball game. The Reverend left for a retreat and conference of pastors. He can't even be reached by phone."

"Really," Cam mused, his brows pulling together in a hint of a frown. "Did he have this planned for a while or was it spur-of-the-moment?"

"I can't tell you. I only know that he isn't in town and won't be for ten days."

"That's going to slow things down. And leave Celeste

under scrutiny even longer if the Reverend witnessed things that could get her off the hook."

"And will admit it," Eden added.

Cam's eyebrows arched, letting her know he agreed that her grandfather would most likely continue to be uncooperative.

"Celeste will need a good criminal defense attorney," Eden said then, thinking out loud.

"We'll make sure she has one."

Eden wasn't sure exactly who the *we* was but she still felt better hearing his reassurance.

It struck her then that his professional position in this situation should have made him the last person to be so adamant about Celeste having legal representation, and from that she began to think about how uncoplike he'd been with Celeste today, too. How calm, kind, considerate and nonjudgmental he'd been. Not at all the kind of cop her late husband was.

"Are you always this way?" she asked him.

He smiled at her. "What way?" he asked, sounding genuinely confused.

"The way you were just now and today, with Celeste, too. Nice. Not intimidating at all."

His smile became a grin, creating lines from the corners of his midnight-blue eyes. "Who did you want me to intimidate? Your grandmother or you?"

Eden smiled back at him. "Neither of us. I'm just saying that in the same situation I'm sure Alika would have been more gung-ho and imposing. For instance— not that today was a good-cop-bad-cop kind of thing— but Alika would never have been the good cop if he were in a good-cop-bad-cop scenario."

"When I was in Detroit I didn't have any problem being bad cop when I needed to be. But here? That isn't called for too often. And I didn't think it was called for today, with a seventy-three-year-old woman I've known all my life."

Still, he'd been impressive in a very low-key manner that Eden had appreciated the same way she'd admired his restraint with her grandfather.

She studied Cam, feeling almost as if she were seeing him in a new light. Maybe she'd been a little off base when she thought she knew his type. Maybe he wasn't so much the way Alika had been. Because while Cam was as physically strong and powerful and capable of a kind of force that could be daunting, he had a nature that required a lot more to ruffle, a lot more to bring to anger.

She liked that about him.

"I'm not sure I've figured you out," she said to him then.

His smile was crooked and devilish as he bent his knees and did a sort of crab crawl to move nearer to her.

"Yeah? Why not?" he asked when he had.

Eden shrugged, suddenly very aware of the feel of her own skin coming into contact with her jeans and the high-neck, button-up flannel shirt she had tucked into them. "I suppose because—a lot like when we were in high school—I always seem to go in thinking you're one way only to find you aren't. And these days you kind of wow me every time I'm with you."

His left knee dropped to the side, landing on her thigh with a welcome, intimate weight. His other knee remained bent, a table for one arm as his top half moved even closer. He made a face that only pretended to be alarmed while his dark eyes let her know he was flattered. "Wowing you every time is a lot to live up to," he said, raising a middle finger to smooth her hair from her shoulder.

"I guess you'll just have to work at it," she challenged, only slightly surprised by the flirtation in her voice when her body was beginning to remember how he'd made her feel the night before.

"I guess I will," he said in a quiet, husky tone of his own as he leaned forward and kissed her.

Two martinis did not make her less fond of the way he kissed. As if his drop-dead good looks, sterling character and delicious personality weren't enough, he could kiss like nobody's business. Eden merely closed her eyes and gave herself over to it, eager to escape the tension of the day, the uncertainty of what was to come.

Her lips parted in answer to his, and her hand raised to his rock-solid chest, absorbing the warmth of him, pleased to discover his pulse picked up speed at her touch.

His hand found the back of her head, his fingers combing through her hair to provide a cradle to catch her when that kiss intensified. His mouth opened a bit more and she went along, meeting and greeting his tongue when it came, welcoming it with glee.

Cam's other arm wrapped around her, pulling her to meet him in the center of the quilt, adding to the depth of the kiss that was rapidly becoming hot and hungry.

Not happy to have her hand keeping her breasts from connecting with his chest, Eden wrapped her arms around him, her hands against his back, closing the gap between them. Her nipples were like pebbles, making her wish for freedom from her clothing.

But it was that wish to be free from her clothing that

had halted things the night before, Eden recalled. That had left her wondering where this would go once clothes had been removed.

Was tonight any different?

It was, but she wasn't sure why. Yes, she knew that the martinis had probably reduced her already over-taxed willpower. But she thought that was the smallest factor. After yet another day of being with him, of seeing more of the complexities of him, of being exposed to another helping of that insidious sensual energy he seemed to unconsciously emit, her feelings for him had just somehow gone over the edge when she hadn't been aware of it.

Tonight was different because as much as she'd wanted him last night, she wanted him even more tonight. And tonight nothing mattered so much as meeting the needs her body was already screaming for, the needs that he'd helped build in her almost from the moment he'd put aside her anger.

His sweater was the bulkiest barrier so that seemed like the first thing that should go. She grasped its hem and began to pull it upward.

But to her surprise, that was enough for Cam to instantly stop kissing her and peer down at her instead.

"I don't think I can take being sent home in the state I was sent home in last night," he warned.

"Who said I was going to send you home?" she asked, kissing the side of his neck.

Then she again looked up into that fine, fine face and found him grinning once more, a flashier, sexier grin than earlier.

"Just so we're on the same page," he said before he

returned to kissing her, a mouths-wide-open kiss that held nothing back now.

Tongues engaged and disengaged, rotated and revolved around each other, did a tip-to-tip flitter, dodged, ducked and parried in a racy dance.

Eden's initial quest to get rid of his sweater was the only interruption and when she'd accomplished that he continued to kiss her as she filled her hands with his broad, naked back, pressing her palms to the silky strength of that expanse, learning every rise and fall, hill and valley of magnificent muscle and bone.

Cam used a more leisurely pace to unfasten the buttons of her blouse, beginning at the top of the high collar. Her breasts were straining against the lace of her bra, against the flannel of her shirt, impatient for the touch of his hand, craving that which they'd had all-too-brief a taste of the previous evening.

It seemed to take hours for him to unbutton her completely and pull her shirttails from where they were tucked into her jeans. And still, just when she was holding her breath with the anticipation of his touch, all he did was slip one hand under the flannel to the side of her waist.

Was there delight in torturing her or did he just not realize how ready she was?

She brought her hands around to his front, finding his nipples and giving him a little of what he was withholding from her. His male nibs responded by forming kernels that couldn't compare to the diamond-hard crests of her breasts and it only made him chuckle low in his throat.

Evil man…

But he wouldn't be hurried and he still didn't do what she wanted. Instead he slid both hands over her shoulders, removing her shirt. Off came her bra, too, unhooked from behind, the straps carried away with only index fingers that managed not to even come into contact with her before he tossed the lacy material aside.

He stopped kissing her then, easing her down to lie flat on the quilt, devouring the sight of her exposed breasts and coming to kiss a shallow path from the hollow of her throat downward, dividing the kisses when he reached the first swell of her breasts, going right, then left, then right again, bringing those feather-light busses to a stop at the very pinnacle of each nipple.

Exquisite torment—that's what it was, heightening her yearning, tightening those ruddy buds to almost painful knots before he finally took one into his mouth and the other into his hand as he stretched out beside her.

He gave equal care and attention to each breast with mouth and tongue, hand and fingers trading off, back and forth. Sucking, seeking. Kneading, caressing. Tightening his hold, increasing his pressure. Releasing his grip and suction. Teasing with circles of tongue and fingertips. Tenderly torturing with delicate pinches and nips. Driving her into a frenzy of need the likes of which she'd never known, bringing her spine off the quilt until it was curved like an archer's bow.

Eden's hands were in his hair, her fingers dug into his back and explored his biceps and shoulders, playing it safe. But playing it safe could only last for so long before she wanted more of him, from him.

Somewhere along the way he'd come to lie mostly over her and so it was easy to find the rear pockets of his jeans, to let her hands glide into them, to the firm mounds of his behind.

Briefly, she mimicked the kneading he was doing. But that pushed his front half in closer, making her aware of the solid ridge hiding behind his zipper. She couldn't be satisfied with only the rear, then. Not when thoughts of something even more delectable tempted her.

She drew her hands out of his pockets, found his waistband and followed it around to unfasten the button that held it closed.

The zipper spread on its own as a magnificent male shaft burgeoned from it. But Eden hadn't even had the chance to grasp it before his hand abandoned her breast and cupped that similar spot on her, his fingers down between her legs.

And despite the fact that his hand was outside of her jeans, it still sent a shock wave of sensations through her that jolted her and made her blood flow faster, carrying with it an increased need.

She found him then, closing her hand around that iron-hard rod she wanted badly now to know, testing the full length of it, making him groan even as he drew her breast so fully into his mouth that it seemed to tighten every nerve ending in her body.

He unfastened and unzipped her jeans then, easing them and her panties down, managing to get them all the way off and toss them aside with very little assistance.

And then his hand was back where it had begun, only without the barricade of her jeans. That hand that was big enough to do astonishing things with fingers had slipped inside of her while his thumb rode higher, moving between her folds, finding that one particular spot and sending her instantly, shockingly, to a peak she'd never expected at that moment. A peak she was afraid might ruin everything by coming too soon until he managed to follow its descent and somehow pull it out of complete decline only to begin a rebuilding.

Breathless and weak and still wanting, Eden lay there nearly helpless as he rose up and shucked the remainder of his clothes. She gorged on that view of majestic man towering there. Glorious, glistening broad shoulders; pectorals taut and cut; narrow waist and tight abs.

He quickly sheathed himself with the protection he retrieved from his jeans pocket and then returned to her. His mouth found hers again, plundering it now, his tongue a saber thrust in divine domination of hers. His hands were on her breasts, their grip one of leashed power that pulled and pushed and worked her flesh even as his fingers gently twisted her nipples into coins of pleasure.

His lower half came to her and she opened her legs to him, thinking, that first climax notwithstanding, if he didn't find his way into her soon she would burst into a million pieces.

And then he did. Slowly, carefully, steadily, but without any inhibition or restraint, he united his body with hers, filling her completely before even more slowly pulling out again.

Not all the way out, though. Almost but not totally before he began the return trip, faster this time, deeper still, even though it hadn't seemed as if he could possibly go any deeper. Then almost out again, then in, until together they were moving, gaining, meeting and drawing apart in a thunderous, pulsing race that ultimately robbed her of his hands so he could brace his weight on outstretched arms. Kissing couldn't continue, either, but so much was coming to life inside her that it didn't matter and Eden just gripped his shoulders and hung on.

He was the driving force with a stamina that made her climb higher than she'd ever fathomed, that built within her a sublime need that gained and gained, that grew and grew until it became bigger than she was. And that was when it hurled her into a zenith that put the earlier one to shame, that rolled her eyes into her head, that brought her up off the quilt to cling to him, that made her see stars exploding into blinding white lights of the purest pleasure.

A pleasure that left her barely able to know that Cam was reaching an apex of his own as his body stiffened and pressed hers to lie flat again, his weight fully on her as he plunged so far inside of her that their bodies seemed to fuse.

Then passion's hold on them both receded, stealing away little by little, inch by inch.

Drained of all but the lingering glow of satiety, Eden relaxed beneath Cam and let her hands fall down his back to his waist.

"I stand by my statement," she whispered when she could, lazily opening her eyes to look at him, struck all over again by just how gorgeous he was.

He kissed her, then dropped his forehead to hers to whisper back, "What statement?"

"That wowing me one."

He pushed into her. "You did some wowing of your own," he assured, sounding as if he might be ready to go again, although Eden couldn't imagine that could be true.

Then he pulled out of her and rolled to lie on his side,

still half on top of her, his arm an arc over her head where he laid his head so that the heat of his breath was in her hair. With his free hand he reached for the edge of the quilt and pulled it over them both, squirreling his arm back underneath it once he had, to drape it over her breasts and hold her close in the protective shelter of his big body.

She felt him truly relaxing then, over her, beside her, above her, and she instinctively wiggled in just a little more.

"I'm not going anywhere tonight," he warned.

"Good," she said because she thought she might have been bereft if he left her.

She felt him pulse again into her side. "But I can't promise to let you sleep the whole time."

Eden smiled and couldn't believe that she suddenly had a renewed craving for him and more of what they'd exhausted themselves with only moments before.

"Okay," she said.

"We should have a nap, though," he suggested.

"We should," she agreed, swiveling her side into him just a little in return and making him groan as his own body began to grow against her.

"Or maybe we could nap later," he mused.

He raised up beside her, leaned over and gave her the sexiest, most arousing kiss she'd ever experienced.

It didn't last long, though.

He ended it to draw the very tip of his tongue down her neck to her shoulder, kissing her there, too. Sucking enough to leave a mark.

Next he followed a course to her breast where his tongue went round and round her nipple, flicking and teasing and tantalizing before he moved on to her navel where he dipped into that just once and then went below. All the way to that spot he'd only recently vacated.

"Oh!" she said as an astonishing third climax took her by surprise to ripple through her just that fast before he settled himself above her once more and began all over again.

Making even the thought of a nap nothing but a distant memory....

Chapter Twelve

Despite the fact that the next day was Sunday and that this was supposed to be his weekend off, Cam's pager sounded at 6:00 a.m., pulling him out of sleep with Eden still in his arms.

The breaking of Celeste Perry's identity was too huge to occur without causing a brouhaha. After kissing Eden's head and whispering that he had to go, Cam didn't have a choice but to ignore his own inclinations and leave her.

The hours that followed were phenomenally hectic. Cam's first order of business was to fill in his fellow Northbridge officers. He'd barely done that when the telephone conferences began. A series of calls from the FBI, the state police and the District Attorney made it clear that there were a multitude of differing views on how Celeste should be handled. The other Northbridge officers agreed with Cam that until it was decided that there actually was evidence against her to warrant an arrest, Celeste should only be under surveillance so she couldn't disappear. Other officials were inclined toward stronger action and because it wasn't ultimately Northbridge's decision, that left the locals in the position Cam had found himself alone in the previous evening, arguing on Celeste's behalf. Which was done, repeatedly and insistently, until they'd won out.

If that wasn't enough, the office was also inundated with drop-ins from residents wanting to know what was happening, contact from numerous newspapers, news stations and reporters looking for interviews and information, and the mayor and entire city council demanding to know what was going on and how it would affect the image of Northbridge.

The entire day was like none Cam had ever spent. Not in Detroit and certainly not in Northbridge. Yet even in the thick of it, his mind was only half there. The remaining half was on Eden.

Because while the day might have been one of a kind, it still couldn't top the night that had preceded it.

The sex with Eden had been through-the-roof-incredible and Cam knew that was part of what still had him stirred up. But as the hours wore on it became clear that the night before hadn't just been about the physical stuff. The physical stuff had just somehow released something in him that was daunting now that it was out there.

Sure, he'd known he was getting to like Eden more and more each time he saw her and that could be risky. He'd known he was attracted to her—hotter than hell for her actually and that, too, could get him into trouble.

He'd known that he enjoyed her company. That she was fun and nothing like he'd thought she was fourteen years ago. And he'd tried to fight wanting to see her, wanting to spend as much time with her as he could, knowing that it was probably a warning sign that he kept losing the battle. A warning sign he should pay attention to.

But after last night?

His eyes were open to the fact that there was more to what was going on between them than he'd realized.

At least on his end. So much more that if what was going on between them didn't have a future, he needed to face that now, before he got in any deeper. Otherwise it could wipe him out. Devastate him. It could be a whole lot worse on him than even his divorce had been.

So he knew he had to think this thing through and figure out just what was going on and where it might be headed. If it was headed anywhere. And by eight o'clock that night, when the situation at the office had calmed down some, he took the opportunity of being formally off duty to finally go home.

The minute he pulled into the driveway the urge to go to Eden's house instead of his own nearly won out. Forget thinking anything through, he just wanted to be with her—that was what flashed through his head.

But he couldn't let himself do that. Not this time.

So he pulled into his garage and then went to his back door without allowing himself a single glance in the direction of her place.

A shower, he needed a shower. And a shave. And food. And some solitary time to think.

Without flipping on any lights, he made his way into the bathroom connected to the master bedroom. He turned on the shower to get it steamy, stripped down and got in, sighing when he'd closed the shower door as if he'd made it through something death-defying and was finally safe.

But now that he felt as if he'd dodged the bullet, he let Eden come into his head again.

Beautiful Eden with her wavy, burnt-sienna hair, her frosted crystal-blue eyes, those lips that tasted sweeter than summer fruit and those long, long legs she'd wrapped around him and used to pull him right into the center of her....

Oh, man, he couldn't think about *that*. Not and ever get to what he *needed* to think about.

He reduced the water temperature to a shocking chill and didn't turn it up again until a shiver shook him and his thoughts were back on target.

Okay, there was no question about how much he wanted her in bed. Or on the floor in front of a fire the way they'd spent the previous night. Wanting her so badly he couldn't see straight and the sexual chemistry between them was not the problem. It was one of the things they had going *for* them.

So what did they have going against them?

A little history, for starters, he acknowledged.

For fourteen years he'd held a grudge against her for making him feel as if he was a lesser life-form—he should probably take a look at that, he told himself, and make certain it *was* history.

Okay, the grudge.

He grabbed the bar of soap and started lathering up.

The grudge had been a whopper, no denying that. Eden had treated him as if he were beneath contempt.

A moron. Too stupid to live. And he'd carried a certain amount of doubt about himself from then on because of it. And resented her as a result. Was he absolutely sure he'd let go of all that?

He considered it.

But when he did, when he looked back on those doubts he'd had about himself, he could see now that he'd worked harder because of them. And because he'd worked hard, he'd moved up the ranks in the army, he'd been accepted on the Detroit police force and moved up those ranks, too. And when he'd wanted to be on the force in Northbridge, they'd jumped at having him, not to mention that since being here he'd turned down offers from the state police four times when they'd tried to lure him away.

Plus, he was more well-read than he probably would have been without that early goading. He'd made sure to keep his computer skills in top form. He'd basically not taken the easy way out of anything again after that physics class. He wasn't sorry for any of that, and in some ways it all tracked back to Eden.

So in a weird way, when he thought of it like that, he actually felt a little grateful to her.

And since her return to Northbridge?

She hadn't treated him anything like she had in high school. Yes, early on he'd been on the lookout for indications that she might still think he was a dimwit, but they hadn't been there. And after he'd relaxed about it? He'd never felt as if he couldn't hold his own with her, or as if he were boring her even if he hadn't talked to her about launching rockets or making research breakthroughs or building bridges—the things she'd said she wanted her next husband to come home and talk about.

But she *had* said that she wanted someone in her life who came home from a nine-to-five job, he recalled. And *that* was the biggest thing working against them—the fact that she didn't want another cop in her life.

No, she obviously hadn't been sticking strictly to that declaration as things between them had escalated, but he knew he had to take it seriously now that they had.

He poured shampoo into his palm and began a firm scrubbing of his hair.

No doubt about it, his being a cop was the biggest thing going against them. It was the single occupation Eden didn't want any part of. The job she knew caused her stress and strain that she didn't want to experience again. The job that had cost her a husband. The job she wanted to be so far away from that she was leaving behind her own successful career to distance herself from everything to do with police work.

That was more of a whopper than the grudge. By far.

In fact, it was a big enough issue to chill him from the inside out and allow him more hot water as he rinsed his hair.

Eden was anticop. Face it, he ordered himself.

Anticop—just as Liz had been. So much like Liz that listening to Eden tell him how she'd felt when her late husband was at work had been almost word for word what Liz had said.

And he already knew he couldn't be happy being anything *but* a cop.

So if that couldn't be dealt with somehow, it was a deal breaker....

He sighed heavily, wishing that wasn't the case.

But it *was* the case and that was the whole purpose

of thinking things through—because if what was against them couldn't be dealt with somehow, he needed to know that now, early on, so he could get out....

He dropped his head back and stepped directly under the shower's spray, standing there, just letting it rain down on him as feelings welled up and told him how much he didn't want his being a cop to be the deal breaker. How much he didn't want the deal broken at all.

How much he wanted Eden.

So damn much...

But where did the cop stuff leave them? he asked himself.

It had left his marriage in divorce court.

But the more he thought of Eden and Liz as alike, the more that idea ate at him.

It just didn't fit.

Eden *wasn't* like Liz. Eden didn't worry over every tiny thing the way Liz had. Eden didn't have that same temperament, the same neurosis that had caused Liz to see mountains in every molehill. Would Eden honestly be freaked out being married to a *Northbridge* cop?

There was no question that Liz would have been, that being a cop *anywhere* would have been too much for her. But maybe Eden just wasn't thinking about the fact that being a cop in Northbridge was different than being a cop in Detroit or Honolulu or any big city. After all, she'd come back to Northbridge *because* it was a calmer, quieter place to live. Shouldn't his being a cop somewhere like that, where less was demanded of the police force, be factored in?

He thought it should be.

But would it?

Reasoning with Liz, doing everything he could to change her mind about his job, hadn't mattered. What if it didn't matter to Eden?

They'd be over before they had a chance.

He didn't even want to think about that.

He turned off the water, grabbed a towel hanging from the bar just outside of the shower and dried off. Then he stepped from the stall and dropped the towel to the bathroom floor, fighting the worry that regardless of *where* he was a cop, his being a cop might sink things with Eden.

He just needed it not to, that's all there was to it.

He needed it so damn bad….

He grasped the sides of the sink and leaned over it, letting his head hang between his shoulders.

"Cut me some slack, Eden," he pleaded as if she were there to hear him.

But the idea that it was Eden—of all people—who had to cut him some slack wasn't reassuring. It left him back where he'd started, to what the grudge had been based on—the way she'd treated him during their tutoring sessions in high school.

Eden hadn't cut him any slack then. She'd lumped him in with other people who had given her a bad time and ended up punishing him for it. And even after she'd seen for herself that he was different than his friends had been, she still hadn't backed off or changed the course she'd put herself on.

"But maybe it won't be like that now," he said, pushing himself away from the sink.

And hoping to high hell that he would be right….

* * *

Was there such a thing as *cautious* ridiculous happiness?

That's what Eden was wondering as she saw Cam through her living room window at nine o'clock Sunday night. He was coming across the front lawn, headed for her house, and that one look at him was all it took for her to feel ridiculously happy.

But she'd been riddled all day long with the worst confusion she'd ever suffered so she knew she couldn't let that ridiculous happiness just run rampant. It had to be tempered.

Making love with Cam the previous night had been unbelievable. While she'd been with him it was as if everything else had been wiped out of existence.

But after he'd left this morning? That's when she'd faced the realities of daylight.

What now? That's what she'd been asking herself ever since.

And she didn't have an answer.

All she had was a body that just wanted another round of what it had experienced last night, a heart that was more full of feelings for Cam than she'd realized and a head that was telling her she had to ignore the other two.

Still, when he rang the doorbell she went to her entryway with her pulse racing with excitement.

"Hi," she greeted when she opened the door, working to curb her enthusiasm.

"Hi," he parroted with what seemed like almost no enthusiasm at all, and a smile that was a bit tight, surprising her.

Even more confused, Eden opened her screen door

and invited Cam in. He accepted the invitation, removing his coat while she closed the front door. But beyond stilted amenities, neither of them said another word.

How could everything have been so smooth and flawless and flowing twenty-four hours ago, and now be so awkward?

"Long day?" she asked, hoping that maybe that's why he lacked zing.

"From six-thirty this morning until after eight tonight. All of it insane," he answered.

He hooked his leather jacket over the hall tree in the corner and Eden watched him. This was not how she'd imagined it would be when she saw him again. She'd pictured him sweeping her into his arms, pulling her close, kissing her hello. She'd thought she would have to be the one to put the brakes on. Instead, even once his coat was disposed of, he made no move to come near her.

He did, however, take a long look at her from the distance and something about that seemed to relax him slightly. The tension eased out of his face, his cobalt-blue eyes warmed, and the smile he gave her this time was more genuine.

But since he still offered only that scrutiny, that smile, she opted for the next question that seemed fitting under the circumstances.

"What's going on with Celeste?"

"Everything is the same with Celeste—she's in her apartment and the state guys are taking turns watching the place. But at *our* office?"

He went on to tell her what had gone on there but Eden was only peripherally listening as she watched him, savoring the sight of him in jeans and a beige crewneck sweater that perfectly cupped that torso her hands were itching to explore all over again.

Then he finished what he'd been saying and she realized they were still standing in the entryway, stiffly, formally, as if they hadn't rolled around on a quilt on the floor all night and slept naked in each other's arms.

But Eden was no more willing to say anything about that than he seemed to be so again she sought refuge in filler.

"Have you eaten?" she asked. "Can I fix you something? Get you something to drink?"

"I haven't eaten, but I don't want anything, thanks," he said.

So why are you here? she wanted to shout.

But she couldn't so she said, "Shall we go into the living room?"

"Yeah," he agreed. "And talk."

That had an ominous ring to it. Was he going to tell her last night had been a mistake?

Not that she hadn't wondered exactly that same thing, in spite of how fabulous it had been. Or maybe because of it.

Was he going to say it could never happen again?

That was something else she'd told herself. Despising the very idea. But maybe she should say it all first.

Except that she couldn't make herself do it....

So she just led him into the living room and sat on the sofa.

He didn't join her there, though, and that was even more unnerving. Instead he propped a hip on the corner of the back of her overstuffed chair, facing her from what seemed like far, far away.

"Is something wrong?" she heard herself blurt out when she just couldn't take the tension any longer.

"You could say that," he answered but in a tone that was quiet, soft, vulnerable.

"Is it about last night?" Again, fear of what he was going to say prompted the question ahead of thought.

"Sort of. Pretty much. Yeah," he answered, sounding as confused as she felt. As she'd felt all day.

This time Eden refrained from speaking and merely waited for him to explain himself.

"Last night was…" He shook his head in awe. "There aren't words to describe last night."

Eden's only response was to raise her eyebrows in part confirmation, part question so he would go on.

"Even in the middle of the worst of what went on today, all I wanted was to be back here. With you. Which was what got me to thinking and asking myself where this is going. Where it can go."

"What now? That's what I've been wondering, too," she said, her own voice quiet.

"Did you come up with anything?"

"No. Did you?"

He took a deep breath and sighed. "Yeah. I realized that I don't want this to go nowhere, Eden," he said as if it were a confession. "It's too good. Too great. And not just last night. Everything that led up to last night, every minute I've been with you, has been… I haven't wanted any of it to end. I think we have something here. I think we could have a whole lot more. And it's what

I want. You're what I want. But I'm worried about what you want. Or what you don't want, actually."

"A cop," she said, her voice a whisper.

"A cop," he confirmed. "So I thought maybe we could talk about my being a cop here, in Northbridge, and how that isn't exactly the same as being a cop other places."

He went on in that vein, obviously trying to convince her that being a law enforcement officer in the small town was not a high-risk occupation.

But even as she listened to him, something was happening to her.

She was forgetting about the night of lovemaking they'd shared, about all the time they'd spent together before that. She was flashing through her years with Alika. Through everything she knew from her own job about the dangers of police work. Through her fears for her late husband and how awful they'd made her feel. How hard it had been to live with them. She was recalling Alika pooh-poohing her concerns for his safety. She was remembering his reassurances that nothing was going to happen to him.

And she was reliving—as if it were yesterday—that one horrible moment when her doorbell rang and there, outside, was her worst fear, her worst nightmare—someone delivering the news that Alika was dead....

At some point—she wasn't even clear when—her head began to shake back and forth.

Seeing it, Cam stopped persuading and said, "What? I *don't* mostly just patrol and keep watch over things?"

"I'm sure you do. But that doesn't mean that's *all* you do. Or all you'll ever do."

"Granted, but in the two years I've been on the force

here I haven't been in a single dangerous situation, Eden. There hasn't been a single dangerous situation for anyone on the force to be in. We check to make sure businesses remember to lock up at night. We give traffic tickets. We tell college kids to keep the noise level down when they're partying and neighbors complain. We—"

"Dig up dead bodies and do investigations into bank robberies and possible murders and answer domestic violence calls and—"

"One dead body and bank robbery that happened well over forty years ago," he qualified. "And yes, there are domestic violence calls and the usual things that happen when human beings are involved, but it's different here. You know that. That's part of why you came back yourself."

"I've done cases in small towns just like this one, Cam. Don't try to tell me things can't happen here because I know they can." And even though she acknowledged that danger might not lurk around every corner, the fact that anything *could* happen was enough to strike terror in her if it meant that the one person she cared for more than anyone in the world was who would deal with it when it did.

"Things can happen anywhere," he countered. "I'm not denying that. I'm just saying the odds are against it in Northbridge."

"It seems to me that the odds are increasing. When we were kids the Northbridge police force was a two-man operation. Now there's four of you. That isn't because Northbridge has become a safer place."

"Primarily it's because the population grew when the college was built. And I know you're going to say that with more people comes more problems, more danger. But Northbridge is still a safer place—by far—than any big city."

He pushed off the seat back and came around the chair, sitting on its arm, closer to her.

He didn't reach for her but he did put both of those big hands on his own thighs and lean forward, closing more of the distance as he said in a gentle voice, "And I'm not the same kind of cop your husband was. I'm not a first-one-through-the-door guy even if something does ever happen here."

Eden felt her eyes well up with tears but she wasn't altogether certain why and she swallowed them back, raising a defiant chin. "You don't have to be a first-one-through-the-door guy to stop a speeder outside of town and have him pull a gun on you and shoot you. You don't have to be a first-one-through-the-door guy to have a drugged-out college kid or an enraged spouse come after you with a knife or a baseball bat or a two-by-four. You don't have to be a first-one-through-the-door guy to have something unexpected happen to you."

"Unexpected things can happen to anybody, Eden. I don't have to be a cop to die in a car accident on my way to church on Sunday, or to roll off the roof fixing a shingle and break my neck, or have a heart attack watching a football game. That's just life."

"Your list is just life. My list adds on to yours when we're talking about cops," she said, hating that her own vulnerability echoed in her tone. "Being a cop doubles or triples or quadruples the possibility that the unexpected—the worst—will happen. And now? Even at my most scared moments worrying about Alika I could talk myself down a little by thinking that I was just being paranoid, that everything would probably be all right. Only I *wasn't* just being paranoid. How could I ever talk myself down again knowing that not only *can* it happen, it did—"

"Because of who your husband was, and how and where he did his job, and because of just plain bad luck. That doesn't mean it will happen to me. Especially not in Northbridge," Cam repeated.

"The place doesn't make that much difference," she insisted.

"It makes a huge difference."

"It doesn't," she argued.

"It does!" he said, frustration raising his voice. "Don't dig in your heels the way you did with me in high school, Eden."

"In high school?" she said, unsure how he was connecting what they were talking about at that moment with something that had occurred fourteen years earlier.

"Yes, in high school. You condemned me for what other people did to you then, and now you're dooming us because you won't open your eyes and see that I'm not the same kind of cop your husband was, and that I don't work in the same environment."

"High school doesn't have anything to do with it," she said, her own voice an octave higher.

"It has everything to do with it if you're turning me down because of what went on with someone else, in some other place, without looking at me, at the way I am, at *where* I am."

He just didn't understand, Eden thought. Because being in the field, in the middle of things, was not the same as sitting at home, wondering and waiting and worrying....

"I can't, Cam. I can't go through it all again. I can't lose you, too," she said.

He searched her eyes with his, his brows pulled into a bewildered frown. "Seriously? Nothing—*nothing*— will put your mind at ease?"

She shook her head definitively. "Nothing."

"And you'd say no to us having any kind of future together rather than just try? Even after last night?" he asked, his voice full of disbelief.

She had to swallow another lump in her throat, thinking again about their night together, looking at that face that she never wanted to glance away from, wanting him, and yet still unable to put herself in the position she'd suffered through once in her life already.

"No cops," she said as forcefully as she could manage. "Never again."

He went on staring at her for a long while, his expression crestfallen but giving her no clue as to what was going through his head.

Then he closed his eyes, took a deep breath and sighed it out as if he'd come very, very unwillingly to some resolution.

When he opened his eyes again the look in them seemed somehow raw and ragged.

"I came over here thinking that either you accepted my being a cop or there was no chance for us because I couldn't be anything else," he said quietly. "But now I'm here with you and I'm picturing a future without you and—" he shook his head again "—I don't want a future without you. So I guess I'll figure out something else to do to make a living. Because making a living at anything else is better than losing you."

At first Eden wasn't sure she'd heard him correctly. She'd been sure he was about to end things with her. But was he actually saying he'd give up his career for her?

"You'd stop being a cop?" she asked dimly.

"If that's what it takes to have you, that's what I'll do."

And work at what? He'd already told her that he'd quit the Detroit force to sell security systems and give seminars in an attempt to save his marriage. And that he'd hated it. That he liked being a cop. That that was all he wanted to do. Which was why he'd gone back to it.

"But you don't *want* to do anything else," she reminded. "And I won't be the reason you stop being a cop. I never asked Alika to stop and I couldn't live with you giving it up for me, either. What kind of a future would we have with that kind of sacrifice hanging over us?"

"A future together," he said with a hint of steel in his tone. "I think anything is worth that."

"But would it always be worth it? Would it be worth it when, day after day, you were doing something you didn't want to be doing? Because I don't think it would be. Not after you've chosen this for yourself *twice* now. Giving up a career because you've decided it's time for that is one thing—that's what I'm doing. But to give up your career—what you love doing—because of someone else's hang-ups? That's something else. And you know it. You've already been there. Unhappily."

"That doesn't mean I'd be unhappy now," he said but without conviction for this decision he'd made so suddenly.

And that lack of conviction was all Eden needed to hear to know what he was proposing honestly couldn't be allowed to happen.

"No," she said again then, with finality.

Cam's handsome face hardened and he drew back, straightening his spine and towering above her from his perch on the arm of the chair. "No? Not even if I'm willing to go this extra mile for you? For us to be together?"

Eden shook her head. "I can't go through being married to another cop no matter *where* he's doing the job, and I won't be responsible for you *not* being a cop when I know that's what you want. So yes, I'm saying no."

"Then what, Eden? We're going to chalk up last night and the time we've spent together as a little fun and now we'll just be plain, old, everyday next-door neighbors? We'll wave when we see each other and just *forget* what we've had here?"

"I guess we'll have to."

"That's the point—we *don't* have to," he said with a note of desperation.

"I think we do," Eden said, holding firm despite the fact that she felt as if she were falling apart inside.

"I don't believe this," he shouted, suddenly getting to his feet, throwing his hands up.

"It's just the way it has to be."

"Because you're too damn stubborn to budge one way or another," he accused.

Eden's shoulders drew back, a little anger of her own asserting itself. "I guess so," she said.

"And that's it? See you around, neighbor?" he challenged.

She nodded. "I'm sorry."

"That seems appropriate," he sneered. "We started this with you apologizing, we might as well end it like that. Too bad you didn't figure anything out in between."

He stormed from her living room and grabbed his coat from the rack with such force that it teetered and landed on only two of its four feet to lean against the wall. Then he threw open the front door and left.

He didn't bother to close the door behind him.

Eden stood and followed the same path to the entry, righting the hall tree, closing the door herself.

Then, like a Thanksgiving parade balloon with the air let out of it, she deflated and sank to the floor, wilting beneath the impact of what she'd just denied herself as happiness—ridiculous or otherwise—deserted her.

And abject misery took its place.

Chapter Thirteen

"Eve. It's almost midnight. What are you doing back here? Is something wrong?" Eden asked her sister when she answered the doorbell that had dragged her away from staring blankly at her television late Tuesday night.

"I saw your light," Eve answered as she stepped over the threshold and closed the door behind her.

"Why were you out? You said you were staying home tonight if I felt like having a sleepover."

"I came to see if you were awake."

"You left your nice warm house this late to see if I was awake?"

Eve shrugged. "I couldn't call and risk disturbing you if you *were* asleep. Not when you haven't slept since Friday night."

Eve knew that Eden hadn't slept in all that time because Eden had told her. After the fight and split with

Cam on Sunday evening, Eden had done what she'd done after Alika's death—she'd withdrawn into herself and gone into seclusion. She'd kept all her curtains and draperies pulled tight, she'd let her phone calls go to voice mail, and she'd sat in front of the TV without caring or paying attention to what was on, crying her eyes into red, puffy ugliness.

But this afternoon, when Eve had become concerned that she hadn't been able to reach her, Eve had shown up, used the spare key Eden had given her and barged in.

Eden hadn't resisted telling her sister the whole story once Eve was there, including the part about the nearly sleepless Saturday night she'd spent making love with Cam. And since Eden hadn't been able to sleep at all on Sunday night after Cam had left, or last night, either, Eve knew that, too.

Still, Eden had the feeling that more was going on with her sister than a drive-by bed check.

"Did you take my advice and soak in a hot bath?" Eve asked.

"I did."

"But you're still awake so obviously it didn't help."

"It felt good, though," Eden allowed.

It had also felt good to wash and condition her hair afterward, which seemed like a tiny move in the right direction. Maybe tomorrow she would even get dressed. Or try to eat…

"You must have put the cold compresses on your eyes, too, because they look better," Eve said, taking a close look.

"Yes, while I was soaking—steamy tub, cold compresses on the eyes, as per your instructions. But you really didn't have to come over at midnight to see if it worked."

"I came to take you for a walk," Eve announced.

So there *was* more to this impromptu nocturnal visit.

"A walk. At midnight," Eden repeated.

"A walk. At midnight," Eve confirmed. "Get out of your bathrobe, put on some clothes and get your coat, it's cold."

"Then why are we going for a midnight walk? Because if it's to help me sleep we might as well not bother. I'm punchy but I don't think even a walk is going to work."

"It isn't to help you sleep."

"Then why are we doing it?"

"Because I said so," Eve decreed.

Eden was too weary and worn-out to argue. Especially since she could tell Eve was determined. And on the off chance that taking a walk in the cold *might* help her sleep, she opted to simply cooperate.

It only took her a few minutes in her bedroom to pull on a pair of jeans, a white hoodie, and some shoes and socks. Then she took her heavy stadium jacket with her to slip into on the return trip to the entryway where Eve was still standing, waiting for her.

Eden held her arms out to her sides and did a pirouette. "Satisfied?"

Eve didn't comment, she merely opened the front door and ushered them out into the night.

"Any particular place we're headed?" Eden asked, hunkering into her coat and putting her hands in her pockets.

"We're just walking," Eve said, heading for the curb.

Eden tried not to glance next door at Cam's house as

she followed her sister. But her traitorous eyes wandered there anyway.

There were no signs of life; the windows were all dark.

He was probably sleeping like a baby, she thought.

But it wasn't resentment of that possibility that put the stab through her heart. It was just thinking about Cam and wanting so badly to be with him....

She blinked rapidly to keep the tears from falling, glad that when she and Eve reached the sidewalk Eve turned in the opposite direction so she didn't have to pass in front of Cam's place.

Relieved by that, at least, Eden took a deep breath of the chilly air in hopes that it would help ease the pain.

"Is this a new exercise regimen or something?" she asked when they were a few houses away and she had some hard-won control again.

"Shh. We're just walking."

Eden was too tired to argue so she just accepted Eve's edict.

They walked in complete silence for a long while. Passed house after sleeping house to Main Street where nothing was open—not even the gas station—and the single traffic light was blinking yellow for the overnight hours. They crossed South Street to the town square where the gazebo was undisturbed and then moved on to the college campus to make a loop that sent them back in the direction of the houses.

All without encountering a car or a truck or another person, seeing not more than a light or two behind a curtained window here and there that announced Northbridge's few night owls.

The air was nippy, but the small town was so quiet,

so peaceful, that that peacefulness began to infect Eden and, for the first time in days, she actually started to feel some of her stress evaporating.

"I forgot that they might as well roll up the sidewalks and take them in for the night around here," she said as they recrossed South Street near the ice-cream parlor and headed toward home.

"Now you remember?" Eve asked.

"Not a lot of action in Northbridge—yes, I remember," she said. Then it occurred to her that maybe that was the point of the walk and she added, "Is that why we're out here—for me to remember that Northbridge is a ghost town late at night?"

"I had to pick up some groceries when I left you this afternoon and I heard some things," Eve said.

If that was an answer to her question, Eden didn't see how. "Okay…" she said. "I'll bite. What did you hear?"

"That Cam is looking to leave the police force. That he's talking to the bank president about managing security for them when old Jeb retires next month. That he talked to the powers-that-be at the college about overseeing campus security. Both jobs on a purely administrative level."

"Because of me?" Eden asked in alarm.

"Nobody knows why. But since I know what went on with the two of you, that would be my guess. I'm figuring that he's thinking if he stops being a cop on his own, then maybe he can get you to agree to be with him."

"Oh no…" Eden groaned.

"You think he has another reason?"

"No. I just don't want him to do that. He won't be happy. It isn't right."

"Do you think it isn't right because whether he is or

isn't a cop you don't want to be with him and he'll be giving up his job for what's only a wild-goose chase? Because I'm behind you a hundred percent if Cam has just gotten carried away, if it's too soon for you after Alika, and Cam isn't seeing that. Or if Cam just doesn't do it for you."

He'd *done it for her* so many times Saturday night she'd lost count. But she *didn't* tell her sister that. Instead she said, "You saw me earlier. You know it isn't that I don't have feelings for Cam or that I don't want to be with him."

"That's what I thought. I think you want him like mad."

Eden didn't respond.

But it didn't keep her sister from continuing as they rounded the corner onto Eden's block.

"I know how you felt being the wife of a cop, Eden. We all worried about Alika but I know it was an everyday thing for you and I also know I wouldn't have wanted to be in your shoes even before he was killed. Then I was there to see how awful it was to bury him, how much you went through. I don't blame you and neither does Faith or any of the family for not wanting to go through that again. But in this situation? I have to tell you that I agree more with Cam than with you."

"But you're behind me a hundred percent," Eden repeated facetiously.

"I am. I'm behind you and I understand. But I hate to see you do something you might regret if your reason isn't valid. Look around—does being a cop here look like risky business?"

So that was the reason for the walk.

"Like I said to Cam—and told you today that I'd said to Cam—things can still happen, even here."

"But they just don't, Eden. Not on the scale they happen other places. I actually went to the library before it closed today and did some research and do you know that no one—not a single Northbridge cop—has ever been killed on the job? And the only injuries have been things like squad cars slipping on the ice in winter and hitting something, or dog bites or once a cop strained his back trying to force the Reverend's garage door open so he could get to Sunday services on time. Oh, and there was one incident where one of the Wallace's horses stepped on a cop's foot at the Founder's Day parade and broke it. But we just aren't talking high crime, Eden."

"Bank robbery and a dead body in the woods aren't low crime, Eve."

"I know. You said that this afternoon, too, and of course you're right. But he's right, too—there's no more risk of him getting hurt or dying on the job here than there is of him getting hurt or dying in the course of living his life anywhere. I'm just saying look around you. Cam is on duty right now—"

Ah, so he wasn't home sleeping….

"Do you honestly think you have reason to worry about his safety?" Eve asked.

"More reason than there is to worry about the safety of someone at home, tucked into bed."

"You really are being kind of stubborn about this, you know?" Eve said, referring to what Eden had told her Cam had remarked during their fight.

"Not fair to use what I told you against me," Eden complained.

They'd reached Eden's house and Eve stopped at her car parked in the driveway.

"You're not coming in?" Eden asked, having thought her sister would.

Eve shook her head. "For your sake and for Cam's, you need to sort through this and think some more about things now that you have the visual—and the statistics—to go with them. But whichever way you decide, will you please talk to Cam before he quits his job if quitting his job still isn't going to get him what he wants? I think he deserves that."

Eden nodded, agreeing with her sister.

"I'll check with you tomorrow," Eve said then.

"Okay," Eden responded. "I'm sorry this whole thing kept you up so late."

Eve waved away her apology and got in her car as Eden let herself into the house.

She really *had* been making a lot of apologies since she'd come back to the small town, she thought, recalling another comment Cam had made. Was she honestly doing so much wrong? she wondered as she hung her coat on the hall tree.

Yes, what she'd done to Cam fourteen years ago had called for an apology. But the others had come from turning him down—directly and, with Eve, indirectly. Were the apologies an indication that she was wrong to reject Cam?

She went into the living room and slumped onto the couch, pressing her hands together between her knees and staring into space as she thought seriously about whether or not nixing a future with Cam now was right or wrong.

Rejecting him hadn't made her feel good, that was for sure. But neither had all the worry and fear for Alika or mourning his death. Having to do any of it again certainly wouldn't make her feel better.

But she knew what both Cam and Eve would say to that. What they'd already said to that—that being a cop in Northbridge wasn't the same, that Cam wasn't the same kind of cop Alika had been.

Did that genuinely make a difference?

It wasn't easy for her to believe that it did. In order to even try, she had to put some effort into disconnecting from her memories of what she'd felt during her marriage to Alika, from things she'd seen and heard over the course of her own work, from the loss of her husband and the thick sea of grief she'd had to swim her way out of.

She did put effort into setting it all aside, though, so she could look objectively at the current situation. At Cam.

Okay, Northbridge wasn't a bubbling cauldron of crime, she admitted. It was a sleepy little hamlet where people were respectful of each other. Where values were strong. Where there wasn't a lot of frustration or turmoil or unfulfilled dreams to cause dissension or conflict or strife. It was essentially a place where people lived because they wanted to, not because there was no way out. They were there because they liked it, because they were happy to be there, so no one caused a lot of trouble.

And if they did? If the police were called in? It helped that everybody knew everybody else. That facing a cop didn't mean facing a nameless stranger with a badge. It meant facing someone it would be embarrassing to face again the next day on Main Street if the behavior got too out of hand.

The statistics were pretty impressive, as well, she had to admit. In view of the fact that no police officer had ever been killed or seriously injured on the job, it was a little more difficult to believe that Cam would be the first. Especially when she'd seen for herself not only how quiet the streets had been tonight, but that the job involved a whole lot more serving than protecting when cops were called to corral a wandering bull or deliver pizza or take a pie out of an oven or find an old man's teeth—all things Cam had done.

And done with good nature, she reminded herself.

It occurred to her that that was important, too. Cam's nature. His temperament.

She'd seen it in action in his dealings with both her grandfather and with Celeste. She'd been impressed with his patience, his kindness, his tolerance. Which, now that she thought about it, had sort of saved her fourteen years ago, too. Anyone else would have lashed out at her during their tutoring sessions when she'd ragged him mercilessly and for no good reason. But Cam hadn't done that. He'd managed to weather it without blowing up at her the way he would have had every right to do.

And if, as a teenager, he could take her abuse without losing his temper, he could certainly take just about anything he might face as a cop and keep control of himself then, too—which she knew could help contain any dangerous situation he might find himself in and keep him out of harm's way.

But containing a situation didn't always help, she reminded herself as doubt crept in. Hadn't he been shot in Detroit in a situation that hadn't waited for containment?

Because the job was unpredictable and it came with a certain amount of danger regardless of where it was being done or who was doing it or how.

So she guessed the question was, could she take it?

Her knees tightened against her hands as just considering putting herself in that position again sent stress running rampant through her body.

It wouldn't be a breeze for me, she thought, recognizing that stress for what it was.

But *could* she take it? she asked herself.

Or should she just sit tight, let him quit being a cop altogether and go to work overseeing security at the bank and the college?

There was some temptation to do just that. But the guilt that came with it let her know that it wasn't an option.

And that meant that her choices were to either stop him from quitting by telling him that whether he was a cop or not, she didn't want him; or to bite the bullet on being in a relationship with another cop.

You can tell him you don't want him no matter what he does for a living, she told herself as if she were giving herself permission.

But then she wouldn't have him.

Just the way she'd been without him since Sunday night.

But the time without him since Sunday night had been almost as bad for her as the time immediately after Alika's death. And realizing that reminded her of the numerous occasions when she'd thought that she would do anything, give anything, to have Alika back. Which, of course, had been impossible. But now, with Cam, it wasn't impossible. She *could* have him back. If only she could accept his being a cop.

She stood and went to the front door again, opening it, peering out her screen, listening.

No sirens. No traffic. Nothing.

And Eve had said Cam was on duty.

He was probably sitting in his office doing paper-work. Or in his SUV, patrolling the same streets she and Eve had safely walked such a short while ago.

It didn't seem scary.

And when he got off duty he'd be coming home to me….

She wanted that so much it hurt.

Too much to ignore.

"Does that mean I just have to bite the bullet?" she asked of the cold night air.

Not even her words disturbed the peace and she wondered if she should take that as a sign.

A sign that yes, she would probably always have some fear, some worry. But that in this peaceful place there wasn't a reason to have as much fear and worry as there had been with Alika. And if there were fewer fears and worries, maybe that would make them easier to live with, easier to calm when they did happen.

And when he got off duty he'd be coming home to me….

She took a deep breath and blew it out, giving in in that instant, knowing the answer.

She wanted Cam in her life, cop or not.

Because what she felt for him was bigger than any fear or worry she'd ever had.

Fear and worry were a small price to pay for having the man.

The man who was willing to give up everything for her.

The man who made her blood rush and her heart pound and her knees go weak.

The man she *had* been wrong to say no to.

And who now needed, once again, to forgive her.

Chapter Fourteen

It was 3:20 Wednesday morning when Eden heard Cam's car pull into his driveway. The hours between midnight and three had given her time to prepare herself.

She'd applied a series of cold compresses to her eyes until every bit of telltale redness had disappeared. She'd done her hair with special care so that it fell around her face in what she hoped were irresistible waves. She'd used a hint of eyeliner, mascara, blush and her best lip gloss. She'd changed from her ratty jeans into a pair that made her rear end look fabulous. She'd also put on a red-as-sin cardigan sweater that she only buttoned from the bottom to the spot right between her breasts where it opened like a deep V and showed cleavage more appropriate for late-night clubbing than for a before-breakfast drop-in.

But no matter what the hour, when she saw Cam again she wanted to knock his socks off.

She gave him a full fifteen minutes after she'd heard his car to get from the garage to the house and settle in. Still, when she arrived at his front door there were lights on, but ringing the doorbell brought no response.

Of course the worst occurred to her—that overnight on the job he'd changed his mind, decided he didn't want anything to do with her after all, and when she rang the bell he somehow knew it was her and just wasn't going to open the door.

But she had to see him, so she rang the bell again.

And again there was no answer.

He might be in the shower, she thought, and if he was she'd be able to see the bathroom light from the back of the house.

She retraced her steps off the porch and rounded the house. As she was walking up the driveway she caught sight of light and movement in the window of Cam's workout room above his garage.

Pausing for a more concentrated look, she realized he wasn't in the shower, he was up there.

Maybe he'd only made a pit stop in the house before going for a workout.

That idea was definitely preferable to thinking that he'd known she was at his front door and ducked out the back to get away from her.

But one way or another, she couldn't wait to talk to him. She'd already nearly gone crazy waiting this long. So she climbed the garage steps and knocked on that door.

To her relief, it opened right away.

"Eden?" Cam said, obviously surprised to see her.

But not too surprised for his dark blue eyes to drop to the cleavage she'd put on display, stalling for a moment before rising to look her in the face again.

"Hi," she greeted, feeling more nervous than she'd expected now that she was with him.

Either he'd gone into the house for a quick change of clothes or he'd done it in the workout room, but his uniform was gone, replaced by only a pair of sweatpants and a black tank top T-shirt that was cut in at the armholes, exposing his shoulders, his biceps and a fair portion of pectorals to advantage.

Once her gaze had strayed to his body, Eden had trouble looking anywhere else. But she reminded herself of why she was here in the first place and forced her eyes to his.

"Can I come in?" she asked.

"Here? Yeah, sure," he said, stepping out of the way so she could enter.

He was using the space strictly for an at-home gym, complete with the bars, weights, machinery, benches and mats that kept him in such good shape.

But it didn't allow for a comfortable place to sit and talk so she went to the window and leaned against the sill, grasping it on either side of her hips for support.

"What can I do for you? Are your lights out again?" he asked when she hadn't found a way to begin.

It helped that he was being so nice to her, that he wasn't showing any signs of lingering anger from their argument.

"No, I wanted to talk to you," she said, much like what he'd said to her on Sunday when he'd first shown up at her place.

He'd closed the door after she'd come in but had stayed near it. Now he moved into the center of the room, near the treadmill, getting up onto it backward and leaning against the handrail. He crossed his arms over his exquisite chest, unconsciously accentuating his biceps where they bulged in the process.

"Okay," he said.

For a moment Eden drew a blank. What was he saying *okay* to?

Maybe she should have tried to get some sleep because it seemed to take her forever to recall that she'd announced that she wanted to talk to him.

When she finally remembered that she said, "Eve was at my house twice yesterday. Part of the reason she came the second time was to tell me that rumor has it you're looking for work with the bank and the college, that you're going to quit the police force."

"I've done some talking," he admitted.

"Because of me?" she asked him quietly.

"Because I meant what I said the other night—I want you more than I want to be a cop."

Oh, she really should have gotten some sleep because that simple candor brought tears to her eyes and she knew exhaustion was contributing to her overly emotional state.

"No," she whispered because it was all she could get out while she battled not to break down.

"*No* again?" he said, his handsome face lined with a frown suddenly. "Is that what you came to say? Dressed like that? No?"

She shook her head, swallowing the lump in her throat and trying to be more articulate. "No, I didn't come to say no again. I came to say no, don't stop being a cop."

"Because even if I do you don't want—"

She shook her head fast and furiously, holding her hands up, palms outward, knowing she was just confusing him further.

"I'm sorry. I haven't slept since…last week."

He took pity on her, stepped off the treadmill and came to take her by the shoulders and move her to the weight bench. "Sit down and just tell me whatever it is you came to tell me," he advised.

She did, perching on the end of the bench as Cam took his hands off her shoulders and hunkered down in front of her.

Trying to ignore how much she regretted the loss of his touch, she took a deep breath and attempted to make more sense. "Eve also made me go for a walk with her. At midnight. To impress upon me how safe Northbridge is. Plus she came armed with some statistic about how no Northbridge cop has ever been killed on duty and the only injuries have been minor. Then she left me to think everything over again."

"And now here you are. Dressed like that…"

It was good to know her change of outfit was having the effect she'd wanted and it produced a small smile.

But she ignored the clothes comment and merely explained all she'd thought about after her sister had gone home.

"I can't say that I'll ever not worry or be afraid. And I may be calling you on duty to make sure you're okay or just showing up somewhere like some crazed, over-protective nutcase—" She took another deep breath and sighed. "But if you promise you won't change your mind and want to get back to being a big city cop, I think I might be able to live with you being a cop here."

"Okay."

It was Eden's turn to frown and repeat his word. "*Okay?* That's it?"

"Here's how it is," he said, taking her hands into his. "Yes, you ticked me off the other night. But that didn't change how I feel about you. I'm in love with you, Eden. And I want to be with you. And nothing is as important as that. So if you have a problem with my being a cop, I'm willing to quit. If you think you can stand it as long as we're here, then we'll stay here. If you ever decide you can't stand it even here, I'll stop. But no matter what, I want you. I want a future with you. I want kids with you. I want a whole damn life with you, and I made up my mind that I'm going to have that. It's good that you came to the same conclusion. But even if you hadn't, I was just going to keep at it until I wore you down."

"So that's it? Just okay, nice that I reached that conclusion on my own and saved you the trouble of wearing me down?"

He grinned and it turned her insides to warm goo. "Yeah," he said confidently.

"Pretty sure of yourself, aren't you, Pratt?"

His grin just got bigger as he released her hands, cupped her hips to slide her farther up the bench so that her legs had to spread to accommodate it, and then rose to straddle it himself, facing her.

"After Saturday night? I knew you felt about me the way I felt about you, and everything else just needed to be worked out."

She decided to give him a bit of a hard time just because he was so cocksure of himself. And of her. "Well, I *like* you, but—"

He stopped her teasing with a kiss, his hands on her thighs, his lips warm and moist and parted over hers, his tongue boldly coming to tempt hers before it disappeared and he ended the kiss.

His hands slid from the front of her thighs to the back, lifting them over his and pulling her more closely to him.

"You more than like me, and we both know it," he said with another show of that self-assurance. "In fact, I'm beginning to wonder if you might have had a secret crush on me in high school and that's why you were so mean—to hide it."

That made her smile again. "I did not have a crush on you in high school. I was terrified of you."

"Terrified and a little hot for me?"

"Just terrified."

He pulled her closer still and proved he was more than a little hot for her right then as the long, steely shaft of him made itself known.

"How about now? Do I still terrify you?" he asked in a voice that had gone deep and sexy.

"Your job, maybe. But you? I think I can handle you," she countered.

"Would you? Please? Now?" he asked incorrigibly, flexing against her.

"Only because you've asked nicely," she said, running her hands up his massive thighs as his mouth took hers once more.

She could have claimed this hadn't been at all in her plan for this middle-of-the-night visit but the fact that she'd forgone both a bra and panties gave her away. Not that they would have made much difference since Cam wasted no time in unbuttoning her sweater and tossing it aside, or standing above her after his impassioned kisses had pressed her to lie back on the bench so he could pull off her jeans.

His own workout wear didn't last much longer and then he brought her up to a sitting position again, this time to straddle him rather than the bench as mouths explored with an unbridled hunger, as his hands found her breasts and reminded her of all they could do to her, as her hands relearned every inch of him and he fitted himself into her as smoothly as if she'd been designed for him.

She'd never guessed that a workout bench could fulfill another purpose quite so well, but with her arms and legs wrapped around him, Cam gave her a demonstration she wasn't likely to ever forget, taking her to ever greater heights of pleasure that left her breathless and spent and almost too tired to be alive.

Her head dropped heavily to his shoulder and the rest of her body draped him as he kissed the side of her neck.

"Are we ever going to do this in a bed?" she whispered.

"I'd say give me an hour but I haven't had a lot of sleep since the last time we did this, either. So maybe give me an hour and thirteen minutes."

That made her laugh even though she barely had the energy for it.

"I love you, Cam," she said then because her heart was just too full not to.

He kissed the uppermost curve of her shoulder. All teasing was missing from his voice when he said, "I love you, too, Eden. Will you marry me?"

"I will," she answered simply.

He reared back so that she had to lift her head from his shoulder, so that he could kiss her mouth again in a sweet, sensual way that seemed to secure their pledge to each other.

Then he lifted her from his lap, stood and leaned over to surprise her by picking her up in his arms and carrying her from the workout room through the dark of night to his house.

"What if somebody sees us?" she whispered as the cold winter air bit her naked body the same way it must have his.

"At this time of night in Northbridge? Not likely. And you're the one who wanted a bed."

Which was exactly where he took her—to his bed, laying her on the softest mattress she'd ever experienced and joining her there to wrap her in his arms and legs and the down quilt that he pulled up to cover them.

"So where are we now?" she asked, teasing him. "An hour and nine minutes?"

"No, I need the full hour and thirteen to sleep," he said as if the time wasn't arbitrary.

"Me, too," Eden conceded, finding blissful comfort against the warmth of that big, honed body, using his chest as her pillow. "Just tell me first that you'll keep yourself safe," she whispered.

He pressed his lips to the top of her head. "You have my word," he vowed sincerely. "Along with the rest of me. Forever and until the end of time."

Maybe it was the fact that she'd had no sleep or that making love with him had put her in a state of such perfect euphoria, but she believed him.

She believed that he would keep himself safe—that he *would* be safe—and that this man she loved more than she could put into words would be hers from that moment on.

And as sleep finally settled over her, she knew without a doubt that regardless of what he did for a living, being with Cam was exactly what she wanted.

Being with Cam.

In the quiet calm of Northbridge.

Until the end of time.

* * * * *

Happily ever after is just the beginning...

Turn the page for a sneak preview of
DANCING ON SUNDAY AFTERNOONS
by
Linda Cardillo

Harlequin Everlasting—Every great love
has a story to tell. ™
A brand-new line from Harlequin Books
launching this February!

Prologue

Giulia D'Orazio
1983

I had two husbands—Paolo and Salvatore.

Salvatore and I were married for thirty-two years. I still live in the house he bought for us; I still sleep in our bed. All around me are the signs of our life together. My bedroom window looks out over the garden he planted. In the middle of the city, he coaxed tomatoes, peppers, zucchini—even grapes for his wine—out of the ground. On weekends, he used to drive up to his cousin's farm in Waterbury and bring back manure. In the winter, he wrapped the peach tree and the fig tree with rags and black rubber hoses against the cold, his massive, coarse hands gentling those trees as if they were his fragile-skinned babies. My neighbor, Dominic Grazza, does that for me now. My boys have no time for the garden.

In the front of the house, Salvatore planted roses. The roses I take care of myself. They are giant, cream-colored, fragrant. In the afternoons, I like to sit out on the porch with my coffee, protected from the eyes of the neighborhood by that curtain of flowers.

Salvatore died in this house thirty-five years ago. In the last months, he lay on the sofa in the parlor so he could be in the middle of everything. Except for the two oldest boys, all the children were still at home and we ate together every evening. Salvatore could see the dining room table from the sofa, and he could hear everything that was said. "I'm not dead, yet," he told me. "I want to know what's going on."

When my first grandchild, Cara, was born, we brought her to him, and he held her on his chest, stroking her tiny head. Sometimes they fell asleep together.

Over on the radiator cover in the corner of the parlor is the portrait Salvatore and I had taken on our twenty-fifth anniversary. This brooch I'm wearing today, with the diamonds—I'm wearing it in the photograph also—Salvatore gave it to me that day. Upstairs on my dresser is a jewelry box filled with necklaces and bracelets and earrings. All from Salvatore.

I am surrounded by the things Salvatore gave me, or did for me. But, God forgive me, as I lie alone now in my bed, it is Paolo I remember.

Paolo left me nothing. Nothing, that is, that my family, especially my sisters, thought had any value. No house. No diamonds. Not even a photograph.

But after he was gone, and I could catch my breath from the pain, I knew that I still had something. In the middle of the night, I sat alone and held them in my hands, reading the words over and over until I heard his voice in my head. I had Paolo's letters.

* * * * *

Be sure to look for
DANCING ON SUNDAY AFTERNOONS
available January 30, 2007.
And look, too, for our other
Everlasting title available,
FALL FROM GRACE by Kristi Gold.

FALL FROM GRACE is a deeply emotional story
of what a long-term love really means.
As Jack and Anne Morgan discover, marriage vows
can be broken—but they can be mended, too.
And the memories of their marriage
have an unexpected power to bring back
a love that never really left....

HARLEQUIN® *Romance*®

What a month!

In February watch for

Rancher and Protector
Part of the Western Weddings miniseries
BY JUDY CHRISTENBERRY

The Boss's Pregnancy Proposal
BY RAYE MORGAN

Also in February, expect
MORE of what you love
as the Harlequin Romance line
increases to six titles per month.

This February…

Catch NASCAR Superstar **Carl Edwards** *in*

SPEED DATING!

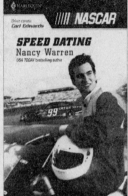

Kendall assesses risk for a living—
so she's the last person you'd
expect to see on the arm of a
race-car driver who thrives on the
unpredictable. But when a bizarre
turn of events—and NASCAR
hotshot Dylan Hargreave—inspire
her to trade in her ever-so-structured
existence for "life in the fast lane"
she starts to feel she might be
on to something!

REQUEST YOUR FREE BOOKS!
2 FREE NOVELS PLUS 2 FREE GIFTS!

SPECIAL EDITION®
Life, Love and Family!

YES! Please send me 2 FREE Silhouette Special Edition® novels and my 2 FREE gifts. After receiving them, if I don't wish to receive any more books, I can return the shipping statement marked "cancel." If I don't cancel, I will receive 6 brand-new novels every month and be billed just $4.24 per book in the U.S., or $4.99 per book in Canada, plus 25¢ shipping and handling per book and applicable taxes, if any*. That's a savings of at least 15% off the cover price! I understand that accepting the 2 free books and gifts places me under no obligation to buy anything. I can always return a shipment and cancel at any time. Even if I never buy another book from Silhouette, the two free books and gifts are mine to keep forever.

235 SDN EEYU   335 SDN EEY6

Name _____ (PLEASE PRINT) _____

Address _____ Apt. _____

City _____ State/Prov. _____ Zip/Postal Code _____

Signature (if under 18, a parent or guardian must sign)

Mail to the **Silhouette Reader Service™**:
IN U.S.A.: P.O. Box 1867, Buffalo, NY 14240-1867
IN CANADA: P.O. Box 609, Fort Erie, Ontario L2A 5X3

Not valid to current Silhouette Special Edition subscribers.

Want to try two free books from another line?
Call 1-800-873-8635 or visit www.morefreebooks.com.

* Terms and prices subject to change without notice. NY residents add applicable sales tax. Canadian residents will be charged applicable provincial taxes and GST. This offer is limited to one order per household. All orders subject to approval. Credit or debit balances in a customer's account(s) may be offset by any other outstanding balance owed by or to the customer. Please allow 4 to 6 weeks for delivery.

Your Privacy: Silhouette is committed to protecting your privacy. Our Privacy Policy is available online at www.eHarlequin.com or upon request from the Reader Service. From time to time we make our lists of customers available to reputable firms who may have a product or service of interest to you. If you would prefer we not share your name and address, please check here. ☐

SSE07

HARLEQUIN®
Super Romance®

Is it really possible to find true love
when you're single…with kids?

Introducing an exciting new five-book miniseries,

SINGLES…WITH KIDS

When Margo almost loses her bistro…and custody of
her children…she realizes a real family is about more
than owning a pretty house and being a perfect mother.
And then there's the new man in her life, Robert…
Like the other single parents in her support group, she
has to make sure he wants the whole package.

Starting in February 2007 with

LOVE AND THE SINGLE MOM
by C.J. Carmichael

(Harlequin Superromance #1398)

ALSO WATCH FOR:

THE SISTER SWITCH Pamela Ford (#1404, on sale March 2007)
ALL-AMERICAN FATHER Anna DeStefano (#1410, on sale April 2007)
THE BEST-KEPT SECRET Melinda Curtis (#1416, on sale May 2007)
BLAME IT ON THE DOG Amy Frazier (#1422, on sale June 2007)

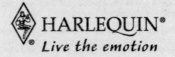

HARLEQUIN®
Live the emotion

Don't miss the first book
in THE ROYALS trilogy:

THE FORBIDDEN PRINCESS
(SD #1780)

by national bestselling author
DAY LECLAIRE

Moments before her loveless royal wedding,
Princess Alyssa was kidnapped by a mysterious man
who'd do anything to stop the ceremony. Even if that
meant marrying the forbidden princess himself!

On sale February 2007 from Silhouette Desire!

THE ROYALS
Stories of scandals and secrets
amidst the most powerful palaces.

Make sure to read the other titles in the series:
THE PRINCE'S MISTRESS
On sale March 2007
THE ROYAL WEDDING NIGHT
On sale April 2007

*Available wherever books are sold, including most
bookstores, supermarkets, discount stores and drugstores.*

COMING NEXT MONTH

#1807 FALLING FOR THE TEXAS TYCOON—Karen Rose Smith
Logan's Legacy Revisited

Skilled at guarding her boss's schedule, twenty-one-year-old office manager Lisa Sanders also had to guard her own heart when Texas real estate mogul Alan Barrett showed up one day without an appointment. But would the secrets of Lisa's wild teenage years derail a runaway romance with this self-assured older man?

#1808 THE PRODIGAL VALENTINE—Karen Templeton
Babies, Inc.

When Ben Vargas returned to Albuquerque to help out with his father's construction business, he was confused as ever about his place in the family and the community. One thing was certain—reuniting with his former flame, sassy shop owner Mercedes Zamora, was a top priority. But would Mercy still want to be his valentine after all these years?

#1809 THE BRIDESMAID'S GIFTS—Gina Wilkins
Businessman Ethan Brannon was in Cabot, Arkansas, to act as best man in his brother's wedding—not to listen to the psychic mumbo jumbo of bridesmaid Aislinn Flaherty. But when Aislinn offered him new hope about an old family tragedy, Ethan had a vision of his own about this compassionate woman and her very special gifts.

#1810 JUST FRIENDS?—Allison Leigh
When producer Leandra Clay enlisted her old friend, veterinarian Evan Taggart, to be on her reality TV series, it was a good match—they were both known to throw themselves into their work. But soon they were throwing themselves into each other's arms…until the show aired, and they suddenly found themselves fending off Evan's female fans!

#1811 THE MARRIAGE SOLUTION—Brenda Harlen
Career woman Tess Lucas knew the night of passion with her best friend, pharmaceutical exec Craig Richmond, was a mistake. Now she had proof—she was pregnant. Yet Tess declined Craig's marriage offer, reasoning their friendship wouldn't survive a thing like *marriage*. Then Craig refused her refusal, and the battle was on….

#1812 FINDING HIS WAY HOME—Barbara Gale
Years ago, heiress Valetta Faraday had fled the family drama of her privileged California upbringing and forged a new path as a reporter in upstate New York. But now Lincoln Cameron was on a mission to bring her back. Would the pretty widow turn the tables and persuade the L.A. playboy to share her small-town life instead?